Lock Down Publications and Ca$h Presents

TRAP STARS

Welcome to Atlanta

I0666783

Written By

B. SHELLY

Lock Down Publications
P.O. Box 944
Stockbridge, GA 30281
www.lockdownpublications.com

Like our page on Facebook: Lock Down Publications
www.facebook.com/lockdownpublications.ldp

Stay Connected with Us!

Text **LOCKDOWN** to 22828 to stay up-to-date with new releases, sneak peaks, contests and more…

Like our page on Facebook:
Lock Down Publications

Join Lock Down Publications/The New Era Reading Group

Visit our website:
www.lockdownpublications.com

Follow us on Instagram:
Lock Down Publications

Email Us: We want to hear from you!

Acknowledgement

First and foremost, I want to thank the Most High for waking me to see another day. Thank you for giving me the strength and the guidance thats needed to keep on keeping on. Thank you for the gift of growth. I'm still growing y'all!

To my family, I love y'all. I'm appreciative for everything to all friends; thanks for the support. To everyone else out there-Peace and Blessings.

To the Lockdown family—thank you for believing in me and my work. I will not let you down. To all my fellow authors, they done messed around and let me in the door! They say good competition is healthy…Lets GO!!

—Shellz

Contact this author…Wilford Shelly-0822320
Email me at GTL GettingOut.com
Or
Send mail at-Text Behind.com

Chapter 1

Drip too hard/Don't stand too close/ you gon fuck around and drown off the wave . . .

The hard lyrics and even harder bassline thundered emphatically from the Bose system as Jewelz pushed the Hellcat heavy around yet another curve. The way the tires gripped and hugged the road, it was like the Charger itself had fallen madly in love with the pavement.

And when he floored the accelerator, the beast opened up — he was definitely turnin' the machine out.

On any given day, that's just how he drove the monster— like it was stolen. The only difference today was, he kept in mind that he was on foreign land. Instead of rupturing the streets of his hometown, Atlanta, he was in central Georgia, tearing up the streets of Macon enroute to see a friend of his, Keisha Armstrong—aka Sugar.

Hitting a hard left, he pressed a button, dialing her number. On the third ring, she answered.

"Hello?"

"Sugar, what's hood? I'm down here by the path now. You ready for me?"

"I'm what's hood, Daddy," she said suggestively. "And I'm always ready for you."

"Tighten up, man. I'm pulling up now."

"Oh Jewelz, I'm already tight. And I need for you to pull up."

"Bye, girl," he said, then pulled in the entrance of the White Plains Projects.

The project was no different than any other low-income housing development in America or any ghetto in the world, for that matter. A few people who truly wanted to do good and make it out, but they were outnumbered by the ones who didn't quite understand how to get out, didn't want to get out, or worse, didn't want you to get out. And of course, it was full of sheisty, grimey individuals who would bust they guns for their hood, without thinkin' twice.

Growing up on the west side of Atlanta, Jewelz understood this dynamic very much. It was what it was until it wasn't. He knew that when they seen his black Charger with the black 24-inch rims come through they, knew who it was. He also knew that some didn't care. Still, not wantin' to spark an all-out state war — and because of who he was — he got a G-pass.

After throwing the Charger in the lot beside Sugar's Tahoe, Jewelz popped in a ruler clip in each of his Glocks.

Next, he grabbed the black bag off the passenger seat and got out. As soon as the rays of the sun lay upon him, his jewelry immediately start performing. The glare from his chain, his watch, and bracelet made him resemble a walking strobe light in the middle of the day. Hence, how Julius Jackson got his street name—Jewelz.

After the second ring of the doorbell, the door swung open, revealing Sugar, in all her glory. Flawless, dark chocolate skin wrapped around a five-foot ten-inch stallion. Her toes were perfectly pedicured as she stood barefoot in a sheer negligee that stopped halfway down her thighs and opened in the front, exposing the valley between her ample D-cup breasts. Her eyes were low, no doubt coming from the aroma of the loud he smelled when the door opened.

However, through all of that temptation, Jewelz's eyes was locked in on the chrome revolver that she held at her side.

"Damn, what—you gon rob a nigga now?" he said, joking as he stepped inside.

"Boy, stop! You know better," she assured while closing the door. "I gotta watch these niggas 'round here. They goofy."

They shared a laugh and gave each other a hug. Always one to seize the moment, Sugar pressed her soft body tight up against Jewelz, allowing him to be aware of her complete nakedness under the flimsy material.

"If ever I rob you, it's gon be for this right here," she whispered in his ear while grabbing hold of his manhood. "Damn, daddy . . . umm, I want this dick." She coaxed him, feeling him grow hard.

Keisha Armstrong aka Sugar. The Chocolate Goddess. Or, as everyone who knew her personally called her, "Bad Bitch." Any of the major strip clubs throughout Georgia that she stepped her stilettos in, she was always the main attraction. However, Magic City is where she called home.

Men and women alike had the game misconstrued when it came to Sugar. They looked at her and saw a fine, thick, talented exotic dancer. What they didn't know was she was also a go-getter, a diva, a boss player with titts. Whatever Sugar wants, by any means necessary, Sugar gets. Anything except Jewelz.

"Come on, Sugar, man. Watch out," he said, pulling back from her skillful touch. "You know I'm still with Jada."

She watched him have to adjust his hard-on before taking a seat on the couch. Smiling, she sashayed her way over to the recliner directly in front of him. Sliding up on the edge of the cushion, she placed one foot on the coffee table, again showcasing her perfect clear and white-tipped pedicure. Then like magic, her thick thighs spread wide open exposing her fresh Brazilian wax job.

"Jewelz, you know you want this juicy pussy. Stop frontin'," she purred while sliding her middle finger deep into her tunnel.

"I know Mrs. Goody Two Shoes, Jada, ain't sucking and fucking you the way a man like you need it," she continued, adding another finger.

Thoroughly entertained, Jewelz watched as Sugar fingered herself right there in front of him. And while it was indeed true that he was faithful to Jada, he was also a man. Two things could be true at the same time.

After feeling himself become more aroused, he had to snatch himself away from her sexual prowess.

"I got that work for you," he said, opening the duffel bag.

Clearly upset, Sugar rolled her eyes then suckered her teeth. Removing her fingers from her juiciness, she put them in her mouth and sucked the nectar completely off.

"Ummm-mmmm good! Boy, you need to try my sugar. It's so sweet!"

When she got up out the chair and went into the kitchen, her cheeks clapped together with each step she took. All he could do was shake his head. This was one of the main reasons that he didn't like coming to Sugar's house. Instead, he let his right-hand man, Envy, take on the task.

Stepping back into the living room, Sugar threw him three bundles of money with thick rubber bands around each one. Not even having to count it, he put it in the bag then gave her some product with two extra ounces.

"Oh, I can get a couple extra zips but can't get no dick . . ." she said, placing her hands on top of her chunked-out hips.

"Aye yo, I'm up. Breathe easy," he said, heading to the door, bag on his shoulder.

"You up? Oh, so you just gon' up and leave?"

"I'm up," he repeated, then headed to his car.

As soon as he backed out the lot, his phone went off. Looking at the screen, he saw "HOME" and he pressed the button.

"Pooh?"

"Julius…" her angelic voice filled the interior of the car. "Where you at, baby?"

Right there in the middle of the street, before he put the car in drive, Jewelz just sat. Something was wrong. Jada knew the kind of business that he was into and understood why he didn't discuss it with her. "Where you at" was one question that she never asked him.

"What's wrong?" he asked with seriousness in his tone.

"Three men came to the house looking for you today. I told them that you weren't here. I've never seen these men before and—"

"Hey. Breathe easy. Slow down. Were they police officers?"

"No. I don't think so. I believe they were African or something. They wore suits and drove black trucks with tinted windows."

That made Jewelz's head snap back with deep curiosity. "African? Suits and black trucks…" he repeated, more to himself than to her.

"Julius, is there anything here at our home that I need to know about?"

"WHAT!" He couldn't believe that she had actually asked him that. "You know I would never bring— I'll be there in a few," he said as he put the car in drive and stood on the accelerator.

The maximum amount of torque hit the back tires so forcefully they spun in rotation, desperately trying to grip the asphalt. Subsequently, the backend fishtailed to the right as smoke covered the entire car before grip was finally caught and the Charger took off like it had been shot out of a cannon.

Jewelz gunned it down Smith Ave in a hurried attempt to get out of White Plains and back to Atlanta to see what was what. His mind had been so wrapped around the conversation he had with Jada that he didn't even notice the man wearing all white standing beside a white G-Wagon, hand in a gun pose pretending to shoot his car.

***

Envy had just got out the shower and was in the process of moisturizing his skin when his phone went off. As soon as he saw the picture of the two familiar faces on the screen, he lit up.

"Yo, what's up with it, mane!"

"West up, that's what's up! Don't play with me! Why ain't nobody heard from you?"

"I been in motion, mane. You know what it do. What's going on in Killa Cali? And which one of y'all this is?"

"You known us your whole life and you still don't know our voices apart? Nigga, you gon' make me crash out on your ass! This Rain. And Compton doing the most right now."

"Rain! Sup wit it! Don't act like that. You know y'all sound just alike," he said, laughing. "Speaking of, where Raven ratchet ass anyway? And Auntie Rachel?"

"Raven is at the house packing and Mom had to move to Portland." She paused for a brief moment. "E, I called to tell you that Mo-Mo got smoked...and uh...me and Raven kind of... found his stash."

All at once the air was sucked out of the room. Envy froze still. There had to have been a mistake. Had to have been. Mo-Mo was a TRUE GANGSTA, a Made Man. Men of Mo-Mo's caliber don't just up and get smoked. He had Compton on smash for the last thirty years. It had to be more to the story.

"How the fuck did that happen?" he asked.

"Uh...I rather not have that conversation on this phone, but what I will say is we gotta move. Right now!"

Envy just shook his head. He did not like what he was hearing. He knew that Mo-Mo was a well-connected man, not only in Compton, but the entire West Coast. He also knew that Mo-Mo had put the twins down with his Immortal Bandit set about five years ago. And now they just up and "kind of found his stash." Something wasn't right.

"I'on't know what's going on, but y'all bring y'all asses out here, mane!"

"We coming, but we can't fly. You know if Raven and Rain coming then so is Queen & Slim! We driving. It'll take a min, but we'll be there."

"Queen & Slim...what the..." He couldn't even formulate his words. "Look, man, call me when y'all step feet in Georgia."

After hanging up his phone, Envy just stared at the wall. His Aunt Rachel and the twins were the only family he had left. He didn't know what had happened out West, but truth be told, it didn't matter. They were family. He would protect them or give his life trying.

He put on his clothes, then headed to the kitchen for a much-needed drink. Downing the first glass, he thought of the situation, then he thought of calling Jewelz. Once the burning effect of the alcohol hit, he poured another and looked at his phone. When the burn from the second round hit his chest, he picked up his phone.

***

It was almost dark by the time Jewelz made it back to the nice, quiet neighborhood in the Buckhead section of Atlanta. This location had been chosen for them by Jada because it was ducked off in the center of the safe and secret suburbs. The move had put her conscience at ease and gave her the deceptive feeling of protection from the nuisances of city life.

Roaring up the driveway, Jewelz came to a sudden halt right beside Jada's Lincoln Navigator. Getting out the car, he slammed the door closed, Glock .40 in hand. While he contemplated this whole ordeal, he stalked maliciously across the front yard, making a beeline straight to the front door. Then suddenly, he stopped.

Slowly, he turned around and allowed his eyes to roam up and down the street. Intensely, he observed his surroundings to see if anything was amiss. As quiet as this neighborhood was, if anything was out of place it would definitely stick out like a sore thumb. After four years of living in Buckhead, Jewelz still hadn't wrapped his head around the calm of the neighborhood. It was a complete one-eighty from the 'jects where he was from.

"Jada! Jada!" he yelled, coming through the front door.

When she didn't answer, he took the stairs two at a time to the top.

"Jada! Ja—" He was cut off when the bathroom door opened and she emerged.

"Julius!" she gasped, running to embrace him. "Are you okay?"

After assuring her that he was indeed okay, they went into the bedroom where he had her explain exactly what had happened. He needed to hear it all again straight from her mouth. He was trying to gauge her level of uneasiness.

"I never seen them before . . . they were different looking . . . they asked for Julius Jackson, not Jewelz . . . they asked for your real name . . . they had black trucks . . ."

"Okay . . . okay, slow down, baby."

The way her words were jumbling together, he could tell she was frightened something serious. And while he himself was not frightened, he was definitely curious as to who these men were and how they knew where he lived. But first things first, he had to calm his lady down.

He stood leaning against the wall while she sat on the bed tapping her foot.

"You scared?"

She looked up to meet his eyes. "No." She lied.

"Jada, how long have we known each other?"

"Since the third grade when you used to sniff my bicycle seat."

Jewelz's head immediately snapped back. "What! What the fuck . . . Where did you get that from? Why would you say that? That's disgusting!"

Jada laughed.

"Girl, you nasty. Don't ever tell nobody that damn lie. Like I'm a perv or some shit. You crazy!" He smiled.

She laughed even harder. But she wasn't fooling him one bit. He knew that laughing was her defense mechanism for when she was scared.

"You right. I knew you since the third grade. No seat sniffing. But I used to bring you candy every day. You still the only person I know who like black jellybeans."

"They're good," she said, still tapping her foot.

"Jada, come here."

Getting off the bed, she walked over to her man. She put her hands around his neck.

"Look at me."

She raised her hazel eyes to meet his.

"I'm good," he told her. "Damn good! I'll never let anyone hurt you. I love you."

It was the tone, the words, and the embrace—all soothed her nerves and alleviated her fears. She had complete faith and trust in him. She knew that she was safe.

"I love you, too . . ."

The moment was interrupted by the unexpected ringing of the doorbell. Jewelz felt Jada's body tense back up.

"Relax," he told her, breaking the embrace and going over to the bedroom window.

Looking out, Jewelz was startled by what he saw. Down in the middle of the street sat a stretch Maybach limousine flanked by two Chevy Suburbans on either side. On his front step stood three men.

Jumping to action, Jewelz pushed the bed over and against the wall. He got down on his knees and knocked on the polished wood floor until he heard a thud. When he heard that, he knew he was in the correct spot.

Using his key, he dug in between two floorboards, lifting one up. Then he did it again, again, and again some more until there was a hole in the bedroom floor.

The doorbell rang again.

Digging inside the hole, Jewelz pulled out his Bushmaster M4 Carbine, two hundred-round drums, and a bulletproof vest. He didn't know who these people were or where they came from, but he knew where he was getting ready to send them.

After strapping on his vest and both drums, he turned to Jada.

"Listen to me. Take these." He gave her his two Glock .40s. "If anyone other than me come through that door, you shoot. You shoot until there's nothing left, like I taught you at the shooting range."

Jada didn't say anything; she just nodded. Jewelz left out the room heading for the stairs. In this part of the game, he fully understood that you kill or be killed. He was not trying to die. He knew how to get busy.

"Julius . . ." she called out, stopping him midway down the steps.

He turned to look at her.

"I love you," she told him.

"You already know!" With that, he slid the bolt back, pulling the rifle on "ready-go" mode. Then he proceeded down the steps.

As soon as he heard the bedroom door upstairs close, he opened the front door and up'ed his M4.

"What's hood!" he said, showing a mouth full of gold teeth.

Three men stood there—all three decked out to the "T" in very expensive suits. Two of them looked like mountains, while the one in the middle was short and squatty. They were most definitely of African descent.

"Mr. Jackson?" asked the man in the middle.

14

"You're not the police or a bill collectors, huh? And you don't look like you work for Georgia Power to me."

The man in the middle smiled. The other two did not.

"Mr. Jackson, I do not work for Georgia Power, and I assure you I'm not the police. My name is Mustafa. I work for a very influential man down in Miami who has been keeping up with you for some time now. My boss is impressed with your special skill set and requires a sit-down at your best convenience."

Taken aback by what he just heard, Jewelz looked at the man who had been talking, then he looked at the two bodyguards standing beside him who hadn't moved an inch or uttered one word. Next, his eyes cast beyond the men to the street where the two Suburbans and Maybach sat waiting. He looked back at Mustafa.

"Who is this man in Miami?"

At that, Mustafa smiled. "Mr. Jackson, I believe you know of the man that I speak of."

He moved his right hand inside the top of his suit. The sudden move caused Jewelz to up the M4 to Mustafa's head.

"Breathe easy," Jewelz told him.

Slowly, Mustafa pulled out a business card. "Please," he said, handing it to Jewelz. "Call this number when you touch down in Miami. When you make the call, you will receive further instructions."

After that, all three men turned and left. Seeing the last truck leave, Jewelz closed the door and went into the living room.

Hearing the front door close, Jada came out of the bedroom and down the steps to see Jewelz sitting on the couch looking at a card.

"What's that?" she asked, taking a seat beside him.

Jewelz looked up from the card, placing his eyes on his lady. Everyone said she resembled Draya Michele, but to him she had her own look. He looked at her eyes, her nose, her mouth. He really loved Jada—he did. But looking at this card and knowing who it came from might just change what they had going on. If things go like he wanted them to go, this might be the opportunity that he'd been waiting his whole life for.

"Pooh, I have to go to Miami."

"What? Why?" she panicked. "Do it have something to do with those men who were here?"

"For business, sweetie."

"Business!" She suddenly stood up. "What business? These men come to our home and you just up and say you going to Miami on business. On business!"

He blew a frustrated breath. "You know I don't speak on the business, and you know why. This might change our life."

She started pacing back and forth. "Okay, but Julius, I want to leave Atlanta. I'm ready to go do more!"

"Jada, what are you talking about? You have nice things, the house you wanted, the car you wanted, a lawyer, and got a man that will die for you. What more do you want?"

She could not believe that he had the audacity to even ask her such a question.

"I want to leave this city that I've been in my whole life! I want marriage, Julius! I want children! I want just one night of not wondering if my man coming home or am I gonna have to go identify his freaking body!" she screamed, falling down on the couch, hands over her face crying.

He looked at her cry for a few seconds. He loved Jada, but she was so emotional. Being that he had learned early in life to keep his emotions in check, her emotional episodes always gave him pause. It was like she had been on the set of *Young and the Restless*.

Getting down on one knee, he lifted her chin so that her flooded eyes were fixed on him. Wiping away her tears, he kissed her lips softly.

"Pooh, listen to me very carefully, okay, because I don't intend on ever saying this again. I love you. I love you more than I ever loved anyone in life. You know my mother died giving birth to me and my father been in the feds since I was eight. You're all I got. But baby, I'm a dope boy—it's who I am.

"Whatever you'll need in life, I will provide. Whatever you want in life, I will get it for you. But I will not stop being a hustler for no one. Not until I'm ready. Now, if you truly love me, then ride with me, Pooh Bear. But if not, there's the door." He said, pointing to the front door.

"I don't want you to leave. But I do want you to be happy. And if in your heart of hearts you're not happy with me, then I will not hold you any longer. Straight up and down. But I am the same guy you fell in love with. This is who I am."

Chapter 2

After having the firm conversation with the love of his life, Jewelz went downstairs to his mancave to watch the game. With Mustafa popping up on his doorstep summoning him to Miami, as well as Jada throwing her temper tantrum, he figured basketball was just what he needed to put his mind at ease.

However, even his Duke Blue Devils throttling the Carolina Tar Heels by thirty-three points wasn't enough to erase the challenging afternoon that had fallen upon him. He really did want to marry Jada and give her children. His desire had been to one day give her the world and everything in it.

While thinking of his happy-ever-after scenario, his phone went off. Seeing Envy's name appear, he pressed the button.

"E, what's hood, Broodie?"

"Sup, mane. What's the business?"

"The business is about to be in motion, I believe," Jewelz told him. "Yo, pull up at Centennial. I getta run some shit by you, my G."

"Yeah," Envy slurred from his umpteenth drink. "I gotta run some shit by you too."

Not only did he not know how to break the news to Jewelz, but he still didn't really know what news to break to him. He himself didn't have the full story. And on top of that, he knew how strongly Jewelz felt for his cousins. It was as if they were Jewelz's cousins as well. He didn't really have too much family, so he loved them and they loved him right back.

"I'm out the door now," Jewelz told him.

"Yeah, I'm getting my keys now."

Thirty minutes later, Jewelz pulled up beside Envy's Dodge Durango at Centennial Olympic Park. Both men exited their vehicles and met in front of the headlights.

"What's hood, homie?" Jewelz embraced Envy. He was instantly aware of his intoxication. Along with his eyes being bloodshot, alcohol was seeping through his pores.

"What's hood, mane," he slurred.

Something was wrong.

"You say you got something to tell me. Yet I see you had to have a couple of drinks first. That lets me know it must be serious. So I'm gon' tell you what I have to say, then we gon' see what you had to get in your cups about just to tell me."

"Bet," Envy said, knowing his partner was super observant on everything.

"So look, we gotta take a trip to Miami, my nigga. Hassan Muhammed sent his underboss, Mustafa, to my crib today."

"You sure?" Envy asked, sparking up a cigarette.

"Look, mane, you know my Glock rock 'til the casket drop, but what's the what with you and Rasheed?"

Rasheed was Hassan's nephew. Two years ago, Rasheed came to Atlanta to party. One of the places on his bucket list was the world-renowned Magic City. When he and his crew entered the club, like mostly all other men on earth, he fell hard when he witnessed Sugar perform.

After throwing close to ten grand on her, Rasheed asked her to be part of his team. While the idea flattered her, she explained that she was loyal to herself only. However, after much inquiring about the chocolate beauty, Rasheed was informed that she had worked for none other than Jewelz.

Not taking the rejection lightly, he told her he could make it where Jewelz don't make no paper. And for three months, that is exactly what happened. He sent a couple of hit squads to other parts of Georgia and told people not to get anything from Atlanta. Being that he was Hassan's nephew, they did as told. When he felt Sugar got the picture, he called off the drought and Jewelz began rolling again.

"Shit, E, that was some years ago. I'm hoping he grew out of that dumb shit and ready to get some paper, you feel me."

"Yeah, I hope so."

"We gon' go check it, tho'." Now he was ready to hear what Envy had to say. "What up, tho'?"

Envy had been thinking of a way to say this, but none had come to him. The only way to say it was to just say it.

"Mane, I think the twins clipped a connected muthafucka out West and they need to get low."

Jewelz took a step back.

"Clipped? Clip like what? Like *clipped*, clipped?"

"Like CLIPPED!" Envy assured.

"What the fuck! Yo, tell them to get out here, man!"

Envy just shook his head.

"Calm down, mane. They on the way. And yo, we gon' handle it."

After dapping each other up, both men got back into their vehicles and went their separate ways. Jewelz went back home to check on Jada. He didn't like the way their last encounter had went down, and he wanted to help comfort her.

Envy, however, did not go home. Instead, he hit up the highway to Macon. To White Plains.

"Sugar, you sure this scale right?"

Bending over, she checked the triple beam. All the measurements were correct.

"Hell, yeah, everything's everything. It's all there."

While she was still bent over, Deon had maneuvered behind her, rubbing himself against her.

"Nigga, if you don't want me to blow that little muthafucka off you, you'll remove it from my ass. Don't play with me."

He snatched the product off the scale, almost spilling it.

"Damn, Sugar, you need to get with the program. Soon I'm gon' be King of Atlanta," he said, full of pride, "and I'm gon need me a Queen."

At that, Sugar laughed. "Nigga, bye! King of what . . . shiiitt! That shit you just got from me belong to Jewelz. The fiends you finna go sell it to belong to Jewelz. The state you are breathing in, belong to Jewelz. Don't get it fucked up!"

He threw the money on the table. "Jewelz? Man, muthafuck-a-Jewelz! This White Plains over here!"

Deon stormed out, slamming the door behind him. After getting into his little Toyota Prius, he peeled out the driveway to the middle of the street.

"Fuck a Jewelz!" he said to himself as he mashed the gas.

When he got to the stop sign at the end of the street, he noticed a black Durango pull into Sugar's driveway. Curiosity got the best of him as he turned around to see who it was.

Riding back to her house, he saw Envy kissing Sugar in a full embrace, hand full of her ass, as she closed the door. That really pissed him off as he kept driving but pulled out his phone.

"Yo, Ghost, that other Atlanta nigga down at that bitch house right now."

"Did you cop the product?"

"Yeah, I got it, but what about this nigga over here at this bitch house?"

"Deon, let me be clear, I don't give a fuck about that nigga! Just bring the product so we can see what we up against. We'll see him on a later date."

"Yeah, a'ight, bet. I'm on the way," he said, heated at the fact that Envy was getting at Sugar instead of him.

Ten days after the twins first called Envy with trouble, they called again — this time to tell him they had arrived. And as soon as Envy pulled up in the parking lot of the Georgia Aquarium, he spotted them. Sitting on triple gold hundred-spoke Daytons in a cherry red '64 Impala on three wheels with the passenger-side tire suspended in the air and the top back were Raven and Rain.

"West up, nigga!" Rain screamed when he pulled up beside them. "Who you be!"

Envy put his hand out the window, holding up three fingers. "U.P.T Third Ward, Magnolia Projects, New Orleans, Louisiana, bitch! Who you be!"

Both twins stood up in the car, threw both hands up, middle and ring fingers crossed, creating a W.

"Westside Crenshaw Immortal Bandits, Compton, California muthafucka!" they screamed.

"Y'all crazy, mane. Follow me."

Thirty minutes later, they pulled into Jewelz's driveway behind Jada's truck. Envy was halfway to the door when he turned around to see the twins standing in the middle of the front yard looking around.

"What's up?" he asked them.

Rain turned her nose up. "Jewelz stay in this white ass neighborhood?"

"Yeah, brah stay here," he assured as they made their way to the front door.

"So . . . we finally get to meet Miss Jada," Raven said sarcastically after Envy rang the doorbell.

Both twins had always had a crush on Jewelz. But where Rain just wanted to sex him, Raven wanted to marry him. Envy made them promise to be respectful. They promised, with their fingers crossed behind their backs.

The door opened.

"What's hood!" an excited Jewelz said, extending his arms.

Envy dapped him up while the twins gave a warm embrace.

When they pulled back, Rain looked at him standing there in basketball shorts and a wife beater on. Her eyes glazed over his tattoos, limitless jewelry, and gold teeth against his jet-black skin, and it made her womanhood instantly get moist. Raven, on the other hand, was mesmerized by his deep waves, his huge crown charm covering his chest — his whole aura had her womanhood going haywire.

"I got burgers on the grill in the back," he said, leading the way.

The twins were taken aback about the classy neighborhood that he stayed in but was even more astonished at the interior of his home. Knowing how hard Jewelz's went in the street one would have never imagined his home to be so beautiful.

Stepping through the glass slide door that led to the backyard the first thing the twins noticed was water. There was a large pond that bordered everyone on Jewelz's side of the street backyard. Along the edges were wood benches and waddling across everyone's yards were ducks. . .

"Damn. Y'all got ducks?" Rain asked.

"Yeah." Jewelz smiled. "We got ducks."

Sipping on pink lemonade at the picnic table, Jada sat under an umbrella taking in the scene. Hearing them talk about ducks, she eyed the twins, wondering exactly what type of women they were.

When she noticed them get a little too handsy touching on Jewelz, she got up to make her presence known.

"Pooh, these are Envy's cousins from Cali that I told you about — Raven and Rain. Ladies, this is my Pooh Bear, Jada."

"It's nice to finally meet you. I've heard so much about you," Jada said, while sliding her arm around Jewelz's waist.

"Nice to meet you, too," Rain said smiling, while Raven said nothing.

Right after they had exchanged pleasantries, the twins eyed Jada and she eyed them right back.

At the young age of only 23, the twins were attractive in a homegirl-down-the-street way. Both had 40-inch braids that traveled down their backs to their very protruding backsides. Their skin was butterscotch brown and seemed to glisten in the sunlight. And standing at only five foot five inches, what they lacked in size was made up for with their fierce heart.

Raven and Rain were two dragons that, if pissed off, would scorch everything in their sights for revenge. Compton bred.

"So what up, what y'all drinking?" Jewelz asked, breaking up the feminine hostility before it started.

Envy told him he wanted Hennessy.

"Raven, Rain?"

"Shit, you know what we want," Raven said, smiling.

"Henny and Patrón, mixed. Bandit style!" her sister chimed in.

"Julius, stay with your friends. I'll get it," she kissed him on the lips. "I'll be back."

As soon as she walked in the house, the twins burst out laughing.

"You call her Pooh Bear?" Raven asked.

"She calls you Julius?" Rain asked.

Jewelz laughed and shook his head. "She don't like the name Jewelz. She knows the streets gave me that name, and since she not from the streets, she won't call me that. So instead, she call me by my government. She the only one who can get away with that tho."

Both the twins' eyebrows raised.

"Excuuuuuuse us!" they said, giving each other a high five.

"Don't act like that," he said, ignoring their play-play attitude. "But damn, it's been awhile! Look at y'all all grown up and shit! Y'all modeling now?"

They walked over to him, invading his personal space. Rain put her hand on his shoulder while Raven slid her arm around his waist.

"Nah, Zaddy, we don't do no modeling. But we do do other things," Rain explained.

"And we do them well," Raven added.

When it came to the twins, there was a stimulating attraction that always seemed to test his devotion to Jada.

In his heart of hearts, he knew it was more than just the twins being fine as hell and thick. He knew that he could have them both at the same damn time.

However, out of respect for his man Envy and his loyalty to his lady, he had never crossed that line with them. Not once. And while all that was a testament to who he was as a man, it definitely didn't stop him from thinking of it.

"I bet y'all do it well," he said, then inched himself away from the poisonous vipers and back toward the grill.

In the kitchen, Jada was putting the drinks on a tray when, looking out the window, she noticed the sisters sticking to her man like two leeches.

The one thing that Jada wasn't when it came to him was naïve. She knew women were constantly throwing themselves at him. They had been doing it since high school.

But now where she lay her head—

"Hell to the nah! Not at my house!"

She finished the drinks and stormed out the door. Next, she put the tray on the table.

Envy went and got his drink. "Thanks, Jada."

The twins moved to get theirs.

"Umm, this what I'm talkin' 'bout!" Raven said, tasting the alcohol. "Yeah, thanks, Joan."

"It's Jada. J-A-D-A," she spelled it out for her with a mean eye roll.

"Oh, my fault, Ja-da."

Jewelz made everyone's plate and set them down on the table. When he went to retrieve his drink, Jada held on to it while looking at him. She was letting him know that she had seen them flirting with him.

He simply smiled and winked at her.

While she loved when he did that, she gave him *that* look.

After eating and drinking more, everybody was good and full and past tipsy. All except Jada.

They talked about everything—except why the twins had come to Georgia.

"Jewelz, you 'member some years ago you came to Compton and them buster ass niggas tried to jack you? No homo!" Rain said, laughing, feeling the effect of her cups.

Envy cut his eye to Jewelz, then to Jada. He knew Jewelz didn't talk about the streets in front of her.

"Rain," he said in an attempt to cut her off, but she was already on a roll.

"When they seen that stick up in that Glock, them niggas ain't know what to do!"

"You talkin' 'bout when y'all first took me to Jack-n-the-Box." Jewelz, too, tried to change the subject.

"Shit, them busters seen all that gold in your mouth and knew you wasn't from the set," Raven butted in. "I'm talmbout, you put plenty holes in they 'Lac!"

"BANDITS!" the twins yelled in unison, at the same time both extending their hands, locking index fingers, then shaking.

"Bitch, I'm smizzy. What we doin' tonight?"

Raven put her cup down on the table, almost spilling it. She looked up at Jewelz.

"I know what I wanna do tonight."

"Yeah, me too. Sho' you right," her other half agreed.

"The club!" Envy announced, interrupting before his drunk-ass cousins said the wrong thing. "Let's go to the club!"

"Pooh, you wanna help welcome Raven and Rain to Georgia?"

He knew she didn't do the whole club thing, but he had to ask anyway.

"No, Julius, I don't. I have to get up in the morning. You go on and go," she said, turning away from him.

"Aww, come on, Joan. It'll be fun!" Raven said while laughing.

Jada had enough. She put her glass down and stood up. She was fed up with these twins.

"My name isn't Joan, it's Jada. In terms where you can understand—like Jadakiss from C-Block. Besides, I have a job. You know, a nine-to-five. I have to get up early."

She looked over to Envy.

"Good night, Da'Shawn."

Then she walked over and gave Jewelz a kiss on the lips.

"If y'all would excuse me, I have to get ready for bed. Nice meeting you."

She then headed back in the house.

"It's D-Block!!" Raven yelled, and she and Rain fell out laughing.

"Bitches," Jada mumbled and closed the door.

"Aye yo! Y'all tighten up, man," Jewelz told them.

"What?" they spoke together.

They all laughed and joked for a little while longer until eventually it was time to go.

Envy had to take the twins to his house on the other side of town so they could get ready for the club.

And Jewelz had to go in and check on Jada to make sure she was good, because he knew this was going to turn into an all-nighter.

***

"Bitch, I'm faded right now. Damn that Henny and Patrón, whew!" Rain said to her sister while turning to get a better angle of herself in the mirror. "My ass is getting too big."

After pulling the straps of an identical skintight catsuit up on her shoulders, Raven walked up to Rain and squeezed her right butt cheek, fingers sinking deep.

"Ummm . . . it's juicy, tho! You done caught up with me."

27

"That's what I said—too big!"

Raven waved her hand. "Bitch, shut up, you sexy!"

"I know! Oh, and speaking on sexy, did you see Jewelz' chocolate ass! That nigga had my va-jay-jay wet as shit!"

"Fall back, mommy. That's my future husband you speakin' on."

"Girl, whatever." She told Raven, "You can marry him. I just wanna fuck."

Raven turned to her sister. "So, you would fuck my husband?"

"Raven, if your husband was Jewelz, you damn right I'd fuck him—and fuck him good, too!"

Together they laughed, followed by their fingers locking in their handshake.

"BANDITS!"

"I just can't believe he with that lame-ass Joan chick."

"No, no," Rain said. "It's Jada, from C-Block."

Again, they laughed hard.

"But nah, seriously, Raven, the bitch is pretty tho' And a lawyer. She got her shit together. And she got to be fuckin' him good—the nigga won't cheat for shit!"

Raven waved her hand. "I on't give a flyin' fuck if she is a lawyer, he need a thugged-out Immortal Bandit on his side. Someone that'll pop out, crash out, up that fire, and drill somethin' for his ass."

Rain just shook her head.

*　*　*

Envy had just got out the shower when his phone went off.

"Sup, mane," he said, throwing a shirt over his head.

"Hey, sexy, can a bitch get dicked down tonight or nah?"

Just the thought of Sugar's tight pussy made Envy's soldier jump.

"Not tonight. I told you my people here and shit."

She wasn't quite willin' to give up that easy. "Damn, Daddy, so you gon' make me beg for the dick?"

"I can't fuck wit' it tonight. Me and Jewelz goin' out of town and . . ." He paused for a minute. "Speakin' of, don't you think it's 'bout time we told Bro we fuckin'? Got me sneakin' around and shit."

Sugar knew that could not happen. As much as she had been tryin' to sex Jewelz, if he found out about her and Envy, in her mind, he would not only *not* sex her but probably cut her pipeline off as well.

She was already takin' a risk sexin' Envy. But at the present moment, it was a risk she was willin' to take. Jewelz and Envy were certified Trap Stars in Georgia, and Sugar refused to be without.

"Not yet, baby. I know how Jewelz feel about datin' a woman in the game. He don't believe in it. I'm just still tryin' to solidify my spot with you."

Envy shook his head.

"Sugar, you know that's my man 50 grand, right? I gotta tell him sooner or later. And what you talkin' datin'? We just fuckin'."

"Nigga, what the fuck ever! Just 'cause I let you fuck whoever you want, you still *my* nigga!"

It was kind of true in a way. She knew Envy was a hoe, but she liked him a lot. And even though he finessed the best "Peaches" in Georgia, for almost two years now Sugar had been the closest thing to his girl.

She was the only lady that he would stay with overnight. He just didn't like the fact that he was hidin' it from Jewelz.

After tellin' her that he'd get at her when he got back, he hung up then dialed Jewelz.

"What's hood, y'all ready?"

"Sup, mane. We ready."

"Bet. I'm gon drive over there, park my shit, and ride with y'all."

Envy chuckled. "Shit, you can ride with me. You know them girls ain't goin' nowhere without that damn six-four."

Jewelz ended the call and put the phone in his pocket. Turning around, his eyes landed on Jada.

Lyin' back against the silk sheet with a light sheen of perspiration covering her whole body, she looked right back at him.

She had that *Got damn, I love you boy!* look plastered all across her face.

That beautiful afterglow was the result of an amazing sexual episode that he had just put her through.

It didn't get past him that she had been in her feelings earlier about the flirtin' that the twins had done right in front of her face. He knew he had to mash the gas and put in some overtime to remind her that it was all about her.

Needless to say, she was well reminded.

Walkin' over, he leaned down and kissed her sweet lips.

"I'll be back later on, Love."

She was still dwindlin' down from the rapture of his lovemakin' that all she could do was nod her head.

However, it was when he was halfway out the bedroom door that her sense of reality kicked in, promptin' her mouth to open.

"Don't forget what I said."

He stopped in his tracks and turned to her. "What's that?"

With her finger, she told him to come here. When he went back to where she lay, she grabbed his manhood through his jeans.

"This is mine!" she told him.

He laughed. "I got you, Pooh."

"Do you love me?" she asked while lookin' up into his eyes.

"With my whole life."

"You better." She smiled.

"You better."

"You better."

They shared a passionate kiss, and then he was out the door.

But Jada just lay there on her back, lookin' up at the ceilin'.

The sound of the front door closing echoed through the house. That's when the tears came.

"Lord, please . . . I love this man. I do. But please help him to stop sellin' drugs. Please! Amen."

Chapter 3

The drive to Savannah had been a short one, considering the way Envy's foot stayed glued to the pedal. Being he already knew how the twins drove, he had no fear of losing them as they stayed damn near connected to his bumper.

Sitting in the passenger seat, Jewelz told Envy that they would be going to Miami in the next three days, so be prepared for anything. He didn't know why he was being sent for by Hassan Muhammed, but he was hopeful that it was to do business together. Either way, he wanted his right hand to be prepared. Envy assured him that he was indeed ready.

Pulling up on Cain Rd, they could see people everywhere. Before they even got to the club, they noticed the line down the block and around the curve. But this was to be expected at *Club Fire*. This was the biggest, most poppin' club on the east side of Georgia.

Chief, the club's owner, was a good friend of Jewelz from years ago. When Chief was first attempting to start the club, it was Jewelz who helped him out financially. In return, Chief gave Jewelz an undisclosed percentage every month.

The twins followed Envy's Durango to the VIP parking lot in the back of the club. After parking, they got out, and the party of four began walking to the front door, passing everyone in the overstretched line. Along the way, scattered excitement started to spread amongst the people.

"Oh shit! Girl, there go Jewelz and Envy!"

"Trap Stars in the building!" someone called out.

"Atlanta on deck!"

Every couple steps, Envy kept stopping to speak and say a few words to some of the women he had smashed all over the Peach State. Jewelz and the twins kept moving. And that's when the inquiry about the two attractive beauties could be heard.

"Damn, who dat?"

"Look, brah, they twins!"

"I ain't never seen them before."

The taut leather material hugged against plump cheeks as the twins did a mean walk in the red-bottom stilettos. Men and women alike couldn't do nothing but stare at the "Gruesome Twosome" as they blessed them with their presence.

After dapping up the bouncers, they entered the front doors. From wall to wall, the club was packed. Local ballers, wannabe ballers, divas, wannabe divas, sluts, thots, goofies, and lames were all in the building. All Jewelz could do was shake his head. He hated clubs. He'd rather be at home, laid up with his woman.

They took a trip upstairs to the VIP section and sat in a large corner booth. He picked this booth so all the action was in front of them and no one would be behind them. As much love as the city of Savannah showed to him, he knew that most of it was only due to the product that his team supplied to them. He knew the love was not authentic. Nor should it have been. He didn't know them, and they didn't know him. It was all business.

They weren't there a full five minutes before two very shapely waitresses came to their booth with two huge bottles in hand.

"From Chief," one said, putting both gallons of Hennessy on the table.

A good hour after they got there, they were all good and feeling it, deep in conversation — and that's when Jewelz's intuition started messing with him. At first, he tried to downplay it. Maybe it was because he was in a club and preferred to be home. Or maybe because of all the alcohol he had consumed from earlier to now.

He tried to shake it off all the way up until he couldn't.

Through the slight intoxication, the music, the smoke, and the crowd, Jewelz made himself focus as he forced his eyes to scan the room. And lo and behold, there it was. Across the VIP was another booth with a party of six people. All were either smiling, talking, or drinking.

All except one.

It was a man decked out in all-white attire, gazing right at him.

The two had locked eyes longer than Jewelz thought necessary before the man blew a big cloud of smoke from a cigarette and turned his head. Jewelz felt the man was a familiar face but could not remember where or put a name to it.

So focused on the man across the room, he hadn't heard Raven talking to him until he felt her patting his arm.

"Jewelz . . . Jewelz! Hello?"

Finally, he came back and turned to her.

"Yeah . . . yeah, what's hood?"

"You good?" she asked, concerned. She really did have a thing for this man.

He wiped his hand across his face.

"Hell yeah. I'm hood, Baby Girl."

"You better be—" Rain butted in, "because we here to have a good time and—"

Suddenly, the club speakers blared:

"Fuckers in school were tellin' me / Always in the barbershop . . . 'Chief Keef ain't about this, Chief Keef ain't about that . . .'"

Rain stopped mid-sentence, lit up with excitement.

"I know damn well that ain't my shit!" she said, on the verge of turning up.

"Motherfuckers talkin' 'bout 'Chief Keef ain't no hitta / Chief Keef ain't this, Chief Keef a fake'. . . Shut the fuck up!"

"Bitch, yes the fuck it is!" Raven said, standing up.

"If I catch another motherfucker talkin' sweet about Chief Keef, I'm fuckin' beatin' they ass! I'm not fuckin' playin' no more . . . You know that nigga roll with Lil Reese and them . . ."

Both the twins screamed and ran to the middle of the dance floor as the beat dropped.

"These bitches love Sosa / O-end or no-end / Fuckin' with them O boys / You gon' get fucked over . . . Raris and Rovers / they do it all for Sosa . . ."

Jewelz and Envy just looked at each other.

Then they looked out to the dance floor and saw Raven and Rain with their hands up, fingers locking and stacking all over the place.

They were definitely in their element.

Envy took that time to speak with Jewelz about the play he was considering.

"So you sho' you wanna fuck with these African cats, mane? I mean, we doin' numbers now."

Jewelz poured himself another drink.

"E, you right — we are definitely doing numbers, but we doing it with product that been stepped on I 'ont know how many times. If we get this connect with purer product, imagine the numbers."

"I feel you, but you don't think they gon' try to high charge us?"

Jewelz was listening to Envy, but his eyes were firmly planted on the twins, who had moved right in front of the table. They went from drilling to Chief Keef to now grinding on one another to Bryson Tiller's *Whatever She Wants*. Both were eyeing him seductively.

"Nah, my nigga. Ain't no high-charging us."

Almost on impulse, Jewelz's eyes darted back to the table with the guy wearing all white. Again, he was looking at Jewelz.

"Jeeewwwelz," Raven called out. "Come here," she said, motioning with her finger.

Turning his head, he saw her and her sister showcasing a mean spectacle — still grinding and fake sexing. As tempting as they looked, his conscience made his eyes revert back to the table with the man in white.

He was gone.

At once, Jewelz stood up, head on a swivel. He looked left, then right — no all white. Leaving the table, he walked around VIP — no all-white. Went down to the lower level, over by the bar — no all white. Pool room, bathroom, dance floor — still no all-white.

It bothered him that he couldn't put a name to the face, but what pissed him off more was the way the dude had kept looking at him.

Content that the man had left the club, Jewelz headed back upstairs to VIP. When he got to the top of the stairs, he heard a loud commotion and immediately looked for Envy and the twins. Then he saw them.

"You touch my ass again, I swear I'll smoke yo' fool ass right where you stand. And that's on my set, nigga!" Rain screamed, pointing in some drunk guy's face.

"Fuck you, bish!" the man said, staggering.

Upon hearing that, Raven's head went back and her eyebrows shot up in amusement.

"Oh hell to the fucking no he didn't," she chuckled. Then, quick as lightning, she snatched up one of the gallon bottles of Hennessy and swung it — hitting the guy across the back of the head. The bottle shattered. Blood and glass flew everywhere. He was out before he hit the floor.

The music cut. Everyone stopped dancing. The lights came on. Then some people from two tables stood up and walked toward Envy and the twins.

"What's up, nigga?" one yelled, throwing his hands in the air.

"Yo! Somebody fuck that bitch up!" said another.

Rain screwed up her face. "I know damn well somebody else did not just call me a bitch. I know not!"

Envy walked in front of the twins, facing the crowd.

"Listen, mane — this nigga here was outta line," he said, pointing to the man bleeding on the floor. "I suggest somebody get his ass outta here."

A couple more people from Atlanta came over to stand on Envy and the twins' side. *Club Fire* had just been divided into two sides.

That's when Jewelz calmly walked up. He looked at the twins.

"Raven, Rain — I need y'all to go outside."

"Fuck that shit. Now it's a muthafucking party?" Rain said.

"Hell yeah! It's time to squabble up!" Raven agreed, wrapping her hair in a ponytail on top her head.

Jewelz only looked at them. Seeing the look in his eyes, they both sucked their teeth, upset.

"Come on, girl," Raven said, grabbing her sister by the arm.

Rain was mad, but she turned to leave.

"Raven, didn't somebody else call me a bitch, tho'?" she asked as they exited the front door.

"Sho the fuck did. And what you gon' do?"

Rain looked into her sister's eyes and smiled.

"You already know."

"Already," Raven smiled back.

Back inside, Jewelz had taken in his surroundings and sized the situation up. This was another reason why he didn't like clubs. Somebody always got drunk and let alcohol get them in a fucked-up predicament.

He turned to the people who had walked up on Envy.

"Look, shit was a misunderstanding. Don't nobody want no smoke, a'ight? We was just trying—"

"Fuck you, Jewelz!" the one in front shouted. "This ain't Atlanta, nigga. This Savannah! You don't run a gotdamn thing down here!"

Jewelz cracked a smile, showing off his gold fronts. Then, without another word, he threw a left straight to the man's stomach that doubled him over — followed by a crushing right hook to his temple. He was snoring before he hit the floor.

One of the guys he was with cocked back to swing on Jewelz, but Envy scooped him and slammed him through a table.

Now it was on. The two sides collided. The club became a Royal Rumble. Even if someone didn't want to fight, they were still getting hit. Bottles, chairs, people — everything was flying.

Pure pandemonium at its finest.

In the middle of it all, Envy grabbed Jewelz by his shirt.

"Come on, mane — before them people get there," he said, speaking about the police.

Not two seconds after that, shots rang out, causing everyone to scatter.

People were stampeding, climbing over one another trying to escape with their lives.

When both men finally made it out the front door, they stopped in their tracks.

Jewelz's mouth opened. His feet turned to lead. His eyes darted left, then right.

Envy pushed him to the pavement — just in time.

In the middle of the street sat the cherry-red six-four Chevy Impala, chrome Daytons sparking under the streetlight.

Raven stood by the hood. Rain stood by the trunk.

Both holding identical Dracos.

Queen-n-Slim.

"PEEK-A-BOO!" Raven yelled, then she and her sister unleashed automatic hell.

The two choppers barked and raged, terrorizing everything in their path.

People were screaming. Gunshots were tinging.

There was nothing Jewelz and Envy could do but keep their heads down as glass rained down around them from the shattered club windows.

After what felt like forever, the clips finally emptied.

Jewelz and Envy jumped to their feet and double-timed it across the street, diving into the backseat of the convertible. The twins jumped in next, hit the gas, and burned rubber getting out of there.

Behind them, a few more shots rang out, causing the fellas to duck again.

In the passenger seat, Raven changed clips, turned around in her seat, took aim, and started hitting again. Three got popped instantly. Everybody else left took off.

Didn't matter. She didn't stop squeezing until they turned the corner and the club was out of sight.

"What the fuck wrong with y'all?" Jewelz asked once they hit the highway. He was thankful, though — him and Envy had left their guns in the truck.

Rain shook her head as she switched lanes.

"Look, I got this . . . this thing about being called a bitch. I 'ont know. Sometimes I just lose it."

Raven turned around to Jewelz and nodded. "Yeah, she ain't lying. That bitch is crazy."

Rain gave her the finger. "Shut up."

"Yo, we gotta go back. I left my truck," Envy said, just thinking about it.

Jewelz told him not to sweat it — he'd call Chief and have him take care of it.

"But I know this little episode gon' cost me big."

"Jewelz, I'm sorry, baby — but that's how we do it on our side," Raven assured.

"The real side," her sister added.

"BANDITS!" they yelled together, locking fingers, throwing the W in the air.

Then they put on Kendrick's *Not Like Us* and hit the gas, rolling up the highway.

Sometimes you gotta pop out and show niggas . . .

Certified Boogeyman . . . I'm the one who upped the score on 'em . . .

The next day, Jewelz and Envy met Chief at the Atlanta city limits. Chief and his wife had come to drop off Envy's truck. Chief explained all the damage: two people wounded from gunshots inside the club, four killed outside, damage from the fighting, and the payouts to keep witnesses from talking to the law.

Jewelz said he understood and apologized. He told Chief to send him the ticket, and he'd double it for all the trouble he had to go through.

After that, they went back to Envy's to get the story on why the twins were really in town.

When they got there, they all went into the living room to talk. Jewelz started.

"Raven, Rain, I appreciate what y'all did last night, but it was reckless. This not Compton. You can't just go uppin' choppers in the middle of the street . . . especially because someone called you a bitch."

Involuntarily, Rain's eyebrows raised.

"But don't think that I'm ungrateful," he continued. "If it wasn't for y'all, we might not've made it to the truck to get the guns. So I'm thanking you at the same time."

"Right now tho'," Envy cut in, "we wanna know what happened out West."

That request made the sisters look at each other before speaking. Then, after a deep breath, Raven started.

"Me and Rain was doin' our thing in Compton — mostly with weed. If you wanted that pressure, pull up on Crenshaw and see the twins. We had quarters, halves, whole pounds — we on deck. And that's loud too, no Reggie!"

"Where the fuck y'all get a sweet-ass connect like that, mane?"

Rain stepped in.

"I met this dude, Tony, from Houston, Texas. We hit it off and started seein' each other. Short story shorter, I find out this fool married with four kids. Fuck it — I start doin' me. He finds out, slaps me, and tells me he'll kill me and the nigga."

Envy jumped to his feet.

"Fuck you mean, he slapped you?"

"Chill out. You know I lined his ass up! I played like I was sorry, stroked his ego and whatnot. This fool not only take me to Houston, but to his stash house. I had already sent Raven there six hours before we got there. Once there, I dropped her the location and left the door open. Forty minutes later, Raven appeared. Can you believe when he saw her holdin' the chopper, the first thing this fucka said was, 'You got a twin?'"

"We tied him up, cut him up, and poured gin in his wounds for like thirty minutes. When he still didn't give up the stash, I put the box cutter under his throat and split him open. Luckily, Raven found his shit on the way out the door. We went back to the set with twenty pounds of Houston skunk and a hundred racks."

Jewelz just sat there listening, nodding. He thought back to last night and how the twins hadn't hesitated when it came time to pop off. That, along with the story he was hearing now, helped him understand a little more just how much the streets of Compton had shaped their lives.

It was definitely more to them than big butts and smiles. They were poison indeed.

"So what happened out West?" he asked.

This time Raven spoke up.

"When we got back, we were high — and I ain't talkin' 'bout no weed. We were on an emotional high. We were definitely feelin' ourselves. So we threw a party and invited the Immortal Bandits to come through. We spread so much love to everybody that night — it was amazing. Anyway, T-Roc, the second in charge, asked us if we gave Mo-Mo any of our shit. I told him we chose to spread love to the soldiers. Mo-Mo stay in Beverly Hills — he straight. The Immortal Bandits didn't sanction this; we did that on our own."

Jewelz understood where they were coming from, but he also understood T-Roc's point of view.

She went on to tell him how the house party got divided — one side saying they should give Mo-Mo something for the lick, and the other side saying they shouldn't have to. Needless to say, it got so thick that the party was shut down before *World War III* broke out.

"The next day, half of the Bandits came over and aired out their grievances about Mo-Mo and how they were sick of how he ran the soldiers — bird-feeding them. But no one had the balls to make a move . . ."

"And since we don't have balls," Rain cut in, "we made the move!"

They put a tracker on his car and learned his day-to-day stops. Parking on the same road where he took his kids to school, they popped the hood, bent over in their miniskirts, and waited. Like clockwork, they saw his Rolls-Royce coming down the street.

Recognizing their Impala, he pulled up to assist. He asked what was wrong. They told him it wouldn't start. Rain asked him to take them to the service station. Looking at their delicious bodies, he told them he had a better idea.

He said, *"Come party with the Don, and I'll buy you a new car."*

"We got in his car — Rain in the back, me in the front. Five minutes down the road, Rain put the .40 to the back of his head and I up'd the Ruger. After that, he took us to his house, where we got two hundred fifty grand and five kilos."

"So after two licks, we had three hundred fifty grand, twenty pounds of skunk, and five birds!" Rain said, full of excitement.

Envy listened to the story, something not sitting right with him.

"So then what happened?"

"We killed him, duh!" Raven laughed. "What you think happened?"

"So, how are y'all in trouble then?"

Raven looked down at her shoes.

Jewelz looked over at Rain.

"Rain . . . what happened? What did y'all miss?"

Rain looked at her sister. Jewelz and Envy exchanged glances — both sensing something was horribly wrong.

Finally, Raven looked up at them.

"Mo-Mo had surveillance all around his house. Me and Rain ain't know this. So when his wife came home and found him dead, of course she called the L.A.P.D. When the cops got there, I guess they viewed the tapes and seen us bring him in at gunpoint. They called the feds."

She shook her head.

"That shit was on every news channel in California. They kicked in Mom's door three times a week lookin' for us."

"When the homies found out it was us, some gave us mad respect. Others wanted blood. Some of Mo-Mo's people put a million-dollar bounty on our heads. We moved Mom to Portland, and we had to get low for the time being."

Envy couldn't believe the feds were lookin' for his cousins for first-degree murder, armed robbery, and kidnapping. He just shook his head.

"Well . . . y'all straight-up outlaws now."

"I know one thing," Raven said as she stood up, "I'll hold court in the street before I let them fuckas capture me."

"Big facts! Six will carry us before twelve judge us!" Rain said, standing beside her sister.

Their fingers locked.

"BANDITS!" they yelled.

Chapter 4

The clock on the wall read 4:30 a.m. Instead of being in his bed asleep, Jewelz was downstairs, sitting on his couch, contemplating the last few days.

First, Mustafa showed up on his doorstep, telling him he needed to go to Miami. Then Envy said the twins had a situation and needed to come to Atlanta. They get here, and not even ten hours in, they go Wild Wild West in the middle of the street.

And now, tomorrow was the day that would either make him or break him.

Either way, he was ready.

"Julius . . ." Her voice was soft, still half asleep.

Turning around, she was there—barefoot, in a red negligée, taut breasts rising then falling. These last couple of days had unsettled her, causing an uneasy feeling.

"Pooh, what are you doing up?"

"I rolled over, and I didn't feel you beside me. So I got up." She took a couple steps around the couch and sat down beside him. "Are you okay?" she asked, staring up into his eyes.

He gave her that smile that made her head spin.

"Yeah, I'm sorry, Bae. I got a lot going on right now, and I got this thing tomorrow. I was just thinkin' it over, that's all."

She grabbed his hands and put them in hers.

"I heard you and Da'Shawn talkin'. I know y'all goin' to Miami for somethin'. Baby, all I ask is that you please be careful and come back to me."

He stood up, then pulled her up to stand in front of him. She put her hands around his neck, and his slid around her waist, pulling her close.

"I'm always careful."

Then, with such ease, he picked her up and she wrapped her legs around his waist. Looking into her eyes, he kissed her soft lips.

"I'll always come back to you."

He carried her upstairs, and they went to bed.

Ten hours after renting a Navigator, Jewelz and Envy hit the streets of Miami. Not wasting any time, Jewelz pulled out his phone and called the number on the card Mustafa had given him.

A woman answered.

"Name?" was all she said.

"Name?"

"Atlanta," he said. He didn't know who was on the other side of this call. He wasn't givin' up his name.

There was a long silence at first. Then finally her voice returned.

"The location—4713 Sunset Blvd. Your presence is required."

Jewelz punched it into the navigation system. Ten minutes later, they pulled up to a large building with two men, as large as WWE wrestlers and black as train smoke, standing at the curb.

When he showed them the card, they told him to pull into the back of the building.

Once they parked, Jewelz looked over at Envy.

"We gon' go in here, have a sit-down with Muhammad, make the connect, and bounce. Brah, stay focused."

Envy put the Mac-11 under his seat but strapped the .45 on his waist.

"Bro, stay focused."

After putting one in the head of each of his Glocks, both men got out and went to the trunk. When Jewelz reached in and pulled out a black Gucci bag holding almost five hundred thousand of his, Envy's, and the twins' money, Envy just looked at him.

Deep down, he felt it. This was their moment. Ride or die. Now or never.

Walking to the back door, they knocked twice, then waited. When the door opened, two more big, blue-black men stepped out—one holding a walkie-talkie, the other a 12-gauge pump shotgun.

The one with the radio spoke.

"You no be here. You go . . ." he was telling them in broken English to leave, until he saw the crown charm covering Jewelz's chest.

He hit the button on the radio. "Him here."

Jewelz and Envy looked at each other. Then the radio cracked back.

"Yes, sir."

He spoke into the radio, then turned to them. "Him wait for you."

They took a step to enter the door when the other man pumped the gauge. Jewelz's eyes cut to the man as he and Envy's hands went to their weapons.

The man with the radio held his hand out, stopping any kind of further action.

"You search before enter."

Envy looked at Jewelz. Jewelz thought hard, but only for a few seconds. He looked at Envy and nodded. Envy knew right then that his friend was willing to sacrifice his life for this connect.

The one with the radio frisked them, pulling out both Jewelz's Glocks and Envy's .45, while his partner held the pump steady.

Next, the bag was checked. Seeing nothing but money, he told them they could enter.

They walked up some stairs, and loud music could be heard. As soon as they went through a set of double doors, Jewelz shook his head.

Another club. And it was jam-packed.

Red lights shined all throughout the club. Women were serving drinks topless and dancing onstage naked.

"Him level two, VIP. Him wait for you," Mr. Radio told them, pointing to another set of stairs.

Before they took a step, he held his hand out to take the Gucci bag.

Jewelz just looked at him. Envy knew Jewelz wasn't about to come off the money without seeing the product.

Mr. Radio told him he couldn't walk through the club with the bag.

To Envy's surprise, Jewelz gave up the bag.

Making it to the top of the steps, they were met by yet two more blue-black WWE wrestlers.

"Boss, there," one said, pointing to a booth.

When they got to the booth, they saw two very beautiful exotic-looking women smiling from ear to ear. In between them was another dark-skinned man. This one was more elegant than any of the other ones they' d previously passed. His black suit was tailored, fitting his form like he was born with it attached to his body. The white button-up underneath, was crisp and on point. His left wrist adorned a gold watch; left hand a single wedding band. The right hand was holding a freshly lit Cohiba cigar with a heavenly blinding pinky ring. Above him stood two more menacing guards staring back at them.

At first sight, Jewelz knew exactly whom this man was. He had seen his picture more than enough times plastered throughout tabloids with the headlines reading: *Mr. Untouchable ' Escapes Federal Charges AGAIN*. In person his power seemed to ooze off of him. This man was none other than, Mr. Hassan Muhamnad.

Hassan Muhammad was the sole leader of one of the most infamous cartels on the planet, the Moroccan Militia. The Moroccan Militia was just as it was named, a militia. It was composed of selected citizens over 1,000 strong that had been trained for warfare from all the nations of Africa banded together under one umbrella for one cause— to protect Hassan Muhammad and his family. On a word they would travel anywhere in the world and take up arms against anyone.

"Gentleman, please, sit," he spoke and with a quick wave of his hand dismissed the two beauties.

They each took a seat opposite Hassan. Both were very aware of his eyes sizing them up.

"I'm delighted to see that the almighty Julius Jackson and his sidekick Da'Shawn Williams could spare the time to come all the way to Miami," he said smiling. "I hope that we will be able to make this trip worth your while. Please join me in a drink."

As they ordered Hennesy the fact that Hassan had just called them by their government names instead of their aliases did not go over their heads. The move was delicate, yet skillful. He was definitely showing his in-depth knowledge, early.

"So, the trip was fine, I hope."

"Only a couple hours. All hood," Jewelz said.

"Did you have any trouble finding the place?"

"No Mr. Muhammad. No trouble at all."

Hassan raised a hand.

"Please, call me Hassan, Julius. Mr. Muhammad is what the feds and someone wanting me to do something for them calls me. Hassan is fine."

"Respect. And you can call me Jewelz."

The waitress came back, put the drinks on the table then left.

"From my understanding, two years ago my nephew, Rasheed, blocked out a little of your friends," Hassan picked back up. "The streets is talking and they say that over half of Atlanta and certain other parts of Georgia belongs to you two. So this must have been painful for you all. I don't know what the beef was about but it must have been serious for Rasheed to act in such a manner. I did not give the order for this, however, he is my brother's son. I love him and support him in the decisions that he makes. What I don't understand is, from what I heard of you two, why was there no retaliation? Please enlighten me on this."

Putting his drink on the table, Jewelz rubbed his hands together letting his rings, watch, and gold bracelet shine in the lights as he got his words together.

"As you know, your nephew runs certain parts of Georgia. I got a female friend that performs at clubs all throughout the state. Well, Rasheed met her at a club one night and offered his services to her. While she was appreciative, she made it clear she was loyal to me. So, not feelin' rejection and wantin' to prove a point, he made moves on my spots."

Hassan took in every word that Jewelz told him.

"So still, why no retaliation?"

Envy looked over at Jewelz. He had asked the same question when he got back from California. Knowing that Jewelz didn't bite his tongue for nobody, he knew Jewelz was 'bout to give Hassan the same answer he gave him.

Envy's stomach tightened.

"I didn't retaliate 'cause I know Rasheed is your nephew. I know who you are, and I respect that. You a man with power, and I respect power. I also respect the fact that you one of the main reasons Georgia is on the map. But I knew if I killed Rasheed, then it would've been a war. Envy was out of town, and I couldn't go to war dolo. And besides that . . ."

Envy's eyes cut up to the bodyguards. He already knew what was comin' next.

"If I killed Rasheed, I knew I'd have to kill you. And I figured you wasn't ready to die just yet."

At once, the mood changed. The tension in the atmosphere was so thick, it could be cut with a knife.

All the guards looked at Hassan Muhammed.

The boss had just been threatened, and they awaited instructions for the retort.

But instead of giving orders, Hassan just looked at Jewelz. For a full ten seconds, he stared—eyes piercing Jewelz's soul.

Then, ever so slowly, a diabolical smile appeared on Hassan's face.

Sitting up straight in his chair, he took a hefty pull off his cigar. Then he tilted his head back, exposing brutal scars from when he was once stabbed and hung—only to survive it all.

He blew out a thick cloud of smoke into the air, mixing with all the tension.

At last, he looked back down at the man across the table who had just told him he would have killed him.

Hassan's smile was gone.

"I must say, I respect you also. I respect your honesty. Honesty is a great virtue to have. You got the eye of a tiger and the heart of a lion. But let me assure you, young one—a war is exactly what it would have been. A war that you cannot win."

"And for that last statement you made—you figured correctly. I'm not ready to die. And I won't anytime soon. Please do not underestimate my power. I can make it rain for a hundred days and a hundred nights. Eventually, you—and anyone you love—*will* get wet. You don't live this long in the game we in on reputation alone. Believe what I tell you."

He turned his attention to Envy.

"Would you have went to war with your friend, knowin' it was me he was goin' to war against?"

Envy squinted, not believin' he just asked that.

"Jewelz is my brother. Point blank, period. I would go to war with him against the Devil."

Again, Hassan smiled.

"I really like the two of you. Both loyal. Both fearless." Then he turned back to Envy. "I believe it's only fair to tell you—the Devil and I been at war for some time now. The score is seven to two . . . my way. So you see, it would *not* have been the Devil y'all went up against. Never mind what you may have heard in the streets—me and my Moroccan Militia are the real deal."

"I understand exactly what you sayin'. But nothin' changes my mind 'bout goin' to war with Jewelz."

Again, studying the two men in front of him, Hassan saw no fear in them. He liked that.

"As I said earlier, I didn't make that call—and it's unacceptable. I will definitely be speaking with my nephew about this. Now, if the two of you would join me, we'll go to Shawtown to further discuss our business."

Envy looked over at Jewelz.

"Excuse me, Hassan, why we goin' to The Shaw?" Jewelz asked.

His hips—where he kept his Glocks—felt naked.

The Shaw was the deadliest project in South Florida. Its reputation was so bad, the police didn't even venture inside. There was a swamp in the back of the projects full of alligators—but they were fenced in. And the saying was true—mess with the projects, and they feed you to the gators.

"It's just where I feel more comfortable discussing business," he said, rising from the booth.

When they exited the back of the club, there were two black Yukon Denalis parked with a stretch Maybach in the middle.

At the back of the Maybach, a man waited with his arms crossed.

"Give them their weapons back," Hassan told one of his guards.

"But sir, I do not think—"

"I didn't ask you what you think. Matter of fact, I didn't ask you anything. Now give them their weapons back."

After receiving the guns and the Gucci bag of money, they hopped in the rental and followed the convoy.

"What you think, E?"

"Shit, I think when Hassan speak with Rasheed, he gon' be mad as hell."

"Fuck Rasheed. I'm talkin' 'bout goin' to *The Shaw*."

"Mane, fuck *The Shaw*! Long as I got my Mac and four-fifth, I'm good."

Jewelz nodded in agreement.

Chapter 5

When they pulled up to the front entrance of the Shawtown Projects, it was like fifteen niggas out front—blunts lit, dice hittin' concrete, bottles clinkin'. Some was blowin' loud, some shootin' dice, others posted up sippin' cheap liquor outta paper bags. But the second them two black Yukons and that stretch Maybach rolled up, shit got real quiet. Dice got snatched up, blunts dropped, bottles slid behind backs. Everybody straightened up. Stood tall.

The Boss was passin' through. Driving into the one-way-in, one-way-out projects, Envy showed Jewelz the men standing on the rooftops of the buildings with walkie-talkies and assault rifles.

"Look, they on they radio alertin' each other that the boss here—with company. Damn, mane, these African cats got shit on lock down here."

As they rode down one of the streets, it looked like a regular project. Children played in the road, sisters braided little sisters' hair on the green boxes, and niggas stood on every corner. The major difference in *this* project was that forty-five percent of Amerikkka's drugs was funneled through this one.

"Holy shit, mane! Now that's some shit you don't see every day."

They pulled up into a cul-de-sac. There, in front of the last building, sat a pink Lamborghini Urus with *BLI2FUL* on the plate.

"A Lamborghini truck in the 'jects?" Jewelz shook his head. "Fuck they got goin' on down here?"

The drivers of the two Yukons got out, hands on their MP5 automatics. They walked to the back of the Maybach, scanning everything that moved. When they were satisfied, one of them knocked on the back window.

The driver of the Maybach stepped out, nickel-plated 9mm in hand. When he opened the back door, Hassan smoothly stepped out. He looked back at the two men in the Navigator and motioned for them to get out.

"Lock and load, my nigga," Jewelz told Envy.

When they all entered the building, it shocked Jewelz to see computers everywhere. The only other things in the room were a big desk with a chair behind it and a black leather couch sitting in front of the desk.

"Please, sit," Hassan said, lowering himself into the chair.

Jewelz's eyes roamed the room, checking for escape routes. The windows were covered with blackout film, and the back door was heavy-duty steel with three deadbolts.

"Now then," Hassan began, "I guess you know the state of Florida belongs to me. Also, the Carolinas, Alabama, Tennessee, Mississippi, Virginia, Georgia, and pieces of Louisiana. In short—everything south of the Mason-Dixon Line. I just choose Florida to lay my head because of the weather and, of course, the women."

Everyone chuckled at that—everyone except the two bodyguards who stood beside Hassan, faces blank and cold.

"Even though I'm African, I got a partner who's Colombian and owes me his life. So, cocaine comes easy for me. I've heard a lot about the two of you. Jewelz, I'd like for you and Envy to come work for me. Atlanta's one place I want my product felt. I was thinkin' of givin' you . . ."

"Excuse me, Hassan," Jewelz said, cutting him off, "that's not why I came here."

A confused look spread across the African's face, and Envy noticed the guards' expressions shift too.

"With no disrespect, I'm my own man. I ain't here to work *for* nobody. I came to work *with* you. I wanna cop from you."

Sitting back in the recliner, Hassan pulled out another cigar. Taking a gold cigar cutter from the desk drawer, he clipped the tip, stuck it between his lips, and waited while one of the guards lit it.

Inhaling deep, he blew the thick, sweet smoke through his nostrils. Through the haze, he studied the two young men and thought about what Jewelz had just said.

A rush of adrenaline coursed through Jewelz as he stared right back at him. He knew Hassan wasn't ready for that offer, but it was out there now. And as much as Jewelz watched him, he understood exactly why Hassan was boss material. Across that man's face was money, power, and respect.

All of a sudden, Hassan's head snapped toward the doorway that led to the kitchen area. The quick movement made Jewelz's killer instinct kick in—his hands flew straight to his Glocks. That, of course, set off a dangerous chain reaction. Envy pulled his .45. The guards responded instantly, MP5s drawn on both men. It was a standoff.

"Uncle Hassan, have you seen my—"

While Envy had his weapon aimed at Hassan, Jewelz stood with both arms outstretched—one Glock on Hassan, the other on the doorway where the voice came from. Then his breath caught.

Through the doorway walked one of the baddest women Jewelz had ever laid eyes on. Red open-toe heels, tight white leggings hugging every curve, and a small red spaghetti-strap top that stopped just above a pierced navel.

Her hair was jet black, long and silky, pulled high into a ponytail tied with red and white ribbons that showed off her flawless face—drop-dead gorgeous, damn near surreal. Her features were superstar-level, her body slim-thick, hourglass perfect. Skin the color of caramel and chestnut blended together, eyes an unreal emerald green. And to top it all off, she was iced out—diamonds from neck to wrist.

Seeing all the guns drawn, she froze in place.

Jewelz turned back toward Hassan, who hadn't moved an inch.

"Gentlemen, please," Hassan said, raising the hand that held his cigar. "This is my niece, Nyomi. Nyomi, this is Jewelz and Envy outta Atlanta."

She looked at both men, then back to her uncle.

"Put your weapons away before somethin' happens that can't be taken back. No one here to kill you. I brought you here to discuss business."

All guns went down, and everyone sat again. Once Hassan was satisfied, he turned toward his niece, who was still standing in the doorway.

"Nyomi, I saw your car outside. What are you doin' here?"

With a fierce model's stride—heels stabbing the tile—she strutted straight to her uncle.

"Rasheed used my laptop and left it here somewhere. I just came by to get it," she said, glancing back at the two men on the couch.

"Hassan, my apologies," Jewelz said. "I just ain't know what to expect."

"I understand your concerns, Jewelz. But why you think I gave you back your weapons? The sense of trust has to begin somewhere. Business or friendship—the foundation of any relationship is trust. If you don't have trust, don't kid yourself—you don't have a relationship."

Envy nodded in agreement, looking over at Jewelz. Hassan had just dropped a hell of a jewel.

"Now, you were sayin'—you wanna buy from me?"

"That's correct," Jewelz replied, his eyes flickin' quick toward Nyomi, who was still watching him.

"Jewelz, while I appreciate your honesty, I don't usually sell to people who not in the Circle of Trust, as we like to call it. However, bein' that I knew you before you even knew yourself, I feel like we gon' be good friends in the near future. I already know you a born hustler, and from today, I see you fearless too. I like that in—"

"Wait, wait, wait . . . what you mean you knew me before I knew myself, and I'm a born hustler?" Jewelz asked, confused.

Hassan smiled.

"Soon enough, you'll know. But for now, I'll give you a deal—16.5 a kilo. You'll be handled by my niece since you and her brother are at odds. In return, all I ask is legit business and loyalty."

Jewelz couldn't believe what he just heard. At 16.5, he could sell a kilo for 25 and make 8.5 profit—or bust it down, ounces for 8, and make back 12.3 profit. Either way, it was a win-win.

"Hassan, the business will always be legit. And loyalty won't be a problem for me or anybody on my team. I won't cross you or your family. And that's on God."

Getting up off the couch, he walked over to the desk and extended his hand. As Hassan gripped it, Jewelz looked at the drug lord.

"Don't put it on God, young one. Put it on me."

That statement caught Jewelz off guard. He'd never heard nobody say that before and didn't know how to respond—but he understood the message.

"I put it on you. I won't cross you or your family."

"Good. Because if you do, I'll kill everything you ever laid eyes on. Then I'll kill you."

After those life-threatening words, the room fell silent. Hassan looked at Jewelz. Envy looked at Jewelz. The guards and Nyomi looked at Jewelz. He didn't say a word. He knew the man in front of him—this man of power—wasn't playin'.

Jewelz just nodded, understanding, then headed back to the couch.

"Wait a minute!" Nyomi chimed in. "I don't know this man!" she said, pointing at Jewelz.

"Nyomi, would I put you in harm's way?"

At that question, she lowered her head in shame. She knew he wouldn't.

"No, Uncle Hassan."

Standing up, Hassan placed his hand under her chin and lifted it up.

"Never bow your head to a man. Not even me." He kissed her on the forehead then declined to the front door with one of the guards on his heels.

"While I have had a grand ole time today, gentlemen, it's time for me to address some more pressing issues. Nyomi and Mustafa here will see to it that you get what you need. It was very nice and interesting meeting you two. Hope to see you soon. Good day."

When the door closed, Jewelz told Envy to go out to the truck and get the money. He went out and came back in with the Gucci bag.

"What exactly are you tryin' to get?" Nyomi asked him.

Jewelz looked up and was just completely stunned by her beauty. He had to catch himself.

"Umm . . . I'm tryin' to get like thirty," he said, pulling out bundles of bills with rubber bands around them.

Nyomi's eyebrow raised.

"Thirty? You know that'll be around . . ."

"Four hundred ninety-five thousand dollars," he said. He'd done the math as soon as Hassan gave him the price.

Nyomi couldn't help but be a little impressed.

"Not many people ride around with half a million dollars in their car."

"Yeah well, one thing for certain and two things fa' sho— I ain't most people."

Nyomi made a confused face.

"What is that, fa' sho? What is that?"

"Oh um . . . how you say . . . You know how most people say 'for sure'? I'm from the South. We say 'fa' sho.'"

"Fa' sho!" he smiled.

Envy noticed the look in Jewelz's eye all too well. It was the same look he gave when he talked to Jada. As much of a beast as he was in the street about his money, he was the total opposite when it came to his woman. Envy knew, deep down, his man was feelin' Nyomi.

"Mustafa," she called out to the guard. "Get the stuff."

When Mustafa went into the other room, Jewelz put the money back in the bag, then looked up at the goddess.

"Mrs. Nyomi, are you gonna give me a number or somethin' so I can contact you?"

Nyomi laughed, and Jewelz loved it.

"Mrs. Nyomi? No, no. Just Nyomi," she told him, still smiling.

Taking his phone, she punched in her number.

"Jewelz, right?"

He nodded.

"So, what's your real name?"

His face changed. He thought that was an off question since they had just met.

"Umm . . . Julius. My friends call me Jewelz because of my love of jewelry. It's just a name the streets gave me when I was little. It just stuck with me."

"Do you mind if I call you Julius?"

The usual request made him cock his head to the side as he looked at her.

"No, I don't mind. But does this mean you don't wanna be my friend?"

"This only means that I like the name Julius better than Jewelz. And actually . . ." she took a step closer, "I was kinda hopin' that you and I could become friends."

With a loud bang of the door slamming, Mustafa came back into the room—two large duffel bags in hand. He set them down on the table in front of Envy. Once he checked it, he let Jewelz know everything was a go.

The four of them walked out the apartment, Nyomi leading the way. As much as he tried not to, Jewelz's eyes couldn't help but land squarely on her backside. She had much bounce with her step, and the way the white leggings wrapped around her ass only made it that much more desirable. Her switch in them heels would make any man stop and stare. She definitely had that energy—just how Jewelz loved it.

While Jewelz and Envy went to the truck, Nyomi went to her Lamborghini with Mustafa by her side. Envy threw the bags in the back, then got in the passenger seat. Jewelz opened the driver's door to get in—but was stopped short by Nyomi callin' his name. She started toward the truck, Mustafa right on her heels.

"Stay," she said, putting a hand up, causing him to stop mid-stride.

"I think I'm gonna need a number where I can get in contact with you as well."

She handed Jewelz her phone.

Under the dim light of the apartment, Nyomi was beautiful. But now—outside, with the radiance from the bright Florida sun hittin' all her seductive features—Jewelz could truly see just how blessedly attractive she really was.

Not wantin' to stare, he started punchin' his number into her phone.

"Your license plate fits you well."

With an adorable touch of shyness, she bit her bottom lip.

"Thank you, Julius. I will definitely be in touch with you."

Getting her phone back, she turned and strutted back to her truck, ass jigglin' the whole way. With an eagle eye, Jewelz peeped the red thong showin' under the white leggings. She got into her truck, and Mustafa got in his Yukon.

Lookin' in her mirror, she saw Jewelz still standin' there with the sun hittin' all his jewelry.

"Yep, I will most definitely be in touch with you, Mr. Jewelz," she said to herself, licked her already glossed lips, then started her engine.

I woke up like this, I woke up like this / Flawless / I woke up like this, I woke up like this / Ladies say, I look so good tonight / Got damn! Got damn! Got damn!

Jewelz smiled and shook his head.

"Hey, mane!" Envy called from inside the truck, snappin' Jewelz out his trance. "You ready or nah?"

When he finally got into the driver's seat, he was about to start the truck when Envy stopped him.

"What's hood?"

"Nigga . . . was that fuckin' Rihanna, brah?!" Envy said, pointin' in the direction Nyomi had just drove off in.

Jewelz laughed as he started the truck.

"Brah, I swear I thought it was. Shawty bad as fuck! She got RiRi's whole vibe—eyes, walk, even the mouth. She look just like RiRi!"

"Mane, you sho that won't her?"

"Nah, brah. They definitely twinnin', tho."

Rollin' back through the projects, Envy turned to Jewelz.

"We got the connect that's gon' take us to the next level. We up now. But peep it . . . why you think Hassan said don't put it on God, put it on him? Fuck he mean by that?"

Jewelz pointed to some of them same men they'd passed when they first entered.

"You see all these niggas he got around here, all on the roof and shit? This the hornets' nest, and these his killer bees. See, if you cross God, He gon' make you pay on His time. Whenever He see fit. But if you cross Hassan? He gon' come get you quick, fast, and in a hurry. He ruthless, my G."

Jewelz knew he had to get closer to him.

***

Before they got back on the road, they decided to hit the mall and spend some more change. They'd heard a lot about Aventura Mall in Miami. Legend has it that it's the largest indoor mall in South Florida, with well over 300 stores. Since they were down there, they figured nothing was gonna stop them from checkin' it out. Not even the 30 bricks sittin' in the back.

The first store they went to was Foot Locker. Jewelz copped two pair of Cool Grey 11s and two pair of "He Got Games." Two for him, two for Jada. Ever since she landed that lawyer gig, all she seemed to wear was heels. But every now and then, she'd throw on some tennis shoes.

Envy bought white-on-white and black-on-black Forces and three pairs of Soldiers. In New Orleans, that's what the dope boys called Reebok Classics—'cause they were light on the feet when you had to get low from the police.

With that Georgia drip and Louisiana lean, people in the mall knew they was from outta town. The men looked at them and respected their gangsta, just like they respected the Florida boys' gangsta. It was universal law—real recognized real.

Jewelz slid into the Chanel store. Inside, women of all shades were browsing racks—Hispanic, white, Black . . . everything. Envy was gettin' ready to say something slick until he caught sight of all that beauty movin' around.

"Excuse me, can I help you with anything?"

They looked up and saw a beautiful woman walkin' their way.

"Naw, shawty, I'm good. But you might be able to help my nigga out, tho."

Jewelz didn't need help. He'd bought enough for them to know their sizes by heart. He left Envy and the saleslady choppin' it up. He already knew—his partner was the one man alive that could pull *any* woman.

Jewelz flipped through a rack of jeans, lookin' for the perfect pair. The ones he wouldn't mind seein' them in. He was on the verge of givin' up and headin' to another store when he spotted *the* ones—right fit, right style. He pulled them off the wall and held them up.

"I don't think those would look too good on you."

He turned around. Red and white ribbons weaved through her hair. Her lips stayed Armor-All glossy. That same mesmerizing smile.

It was Nyomi. Emerald green eyes lookin' straight through his soul.

"These ain't for me."

She took the jeans out his hands and held them up. "I hope not." Then tilted her head, curiosity in her eyes. "For your girlfriend then?"

"Nah. Not my girlfriend."

"She's not your girlfriend . . . or you don't *have* a girlfriend?"

"She's not my girlfriend."

She placed a hand on her hip. "So you want me to believe you *don't* have a girlfriend?"

"No."

"No, you don't want me to believe that you *don't* have a girlfriend, or no, you *don't* have a girlfriend?"

"No, I don't want you to believe that I don't have a girlfriend."

That made her raise an eyebrow. "Oh! So you want me to believe that you *do* have a girlfriend . . . but you really don't?"

"No."

"No, you don't want me to believe that, or no, you don't have a girlfriend?"

Lightly, Jewelz grabbed the jeans from her hands. "These jeans is for a friend."

"If you say so. I thought you'd be back on your way to Atlanta by now."

"I heard a lot about this mall. Had to check it out, tho. But once we leave here—it's Atlanta bound. You came to get somethin' for your man?"

She rolled her eyes. "No."

He decided to have a little fun.

"No, you didn't come to pick somethin' up, or no, not for your man?"

"Yes, I came to pick somethin' up . . . but not for my man."

Jewelz folded the jeans over his arm. "You want me to believe somebody as beautiful as you don't got a man?"

"No."

"No, you don't want me to believe that you don't have a man, or no, you don't have a man?"

Realizin' what he was doin' made her laugh out loud. And that laugh? That sparked a chain reaction—made *him* laugh, too. In that moment, she noticed just how attractive he really was. Her laugh faded. She stepped closer.

"Julius . . . I don't have a man. I haven't had a boyfriend since I was 17. That was eight years ago."

"What . . . why?"

"A couple of guys I found attractive ran off when they found out who my brother and uncle are. And anybody else . . . well . . . I just never had the nerve to approach."

He understood the first part. But definitely not the last.

"You ain't had the nerve to . . . what? Come on now. Beautiful as you are?"

She placed her hands on his shoulder.

"Julius, that's the third time today you've called me beautiful. I appreciate the compliment . . . I'm just not too experienced when it comes to men," she said, lowering her head.

With the palm of his hand, he lifted her chin so they were eye to eye.

"That's nothin' to be ashamed of."

Envy came up behind Jewelz, not seein' Nyomi.

"Aye, mane! We gotta come back to Miami. You know how many numbers I got? I'm definitely gon' be flippin' these bite—"

He saw her.

Nyomi backed away from Jewelz's hand.

"Hello again, Envy."

"Rihanna?" he asked. Jewelz shook his head.

"What?" she asked, confused.

"Nothin', man," Jewelz said. "He ain't talkin' 'bout nothin'."

"Hey, mane, I had to see for myself." Again, Jewelz shook his head.

"Envy . . . do Julius have a girlfriend?"

The question caught him way off guard. His eyes went to Jewelz, then to Nyomi, then back to Jewelz again. He opened his mouth . . . but nothin' came out.

When he didn't answer, she had all the answer she needed.

"Thanks," she said, patting Envy on the shoulder. "See y'all when it's time to re-up."

She turned and walked right out the store.

Envy looked at Jewelz.

"Damn, mane . . . what's that 'bout? What you done did?"

"Ain't nothin', my nigga. Come on, let's get the hell outta here."

At the register, Jewelz couldn't help it.

"Why you call that woman Rihanna, brah?"

"Shiiit! I know you said it wasn't her, but I had to see for myself. Damn . . . they twins!"

On the way out the mall, Jewelz made one more stop. A pet store with a big-ass German Rottweiler in the window. He had to have him.

"I'm sorry, sir. He ain't for sale."

Turnin' around, they saw a light-skinned woman with *Yolonda* on her tag.

"Why not?" Envy asked, smiling.

65

Like most women who'd seen his smile, her heart skipped a beat.

"We've had him for a while . . . and he don't like nobody."

"Well, I want him."

"I'm sorry, sir."

Envy asked if he could speak to her in private. While they walked toward the back of the store, Jewelz made friends with the dog. Kneeling down, he stuck his hand through the cage. The Rottweiler started to growl but he kept his hand steady. Even when he jumped at the hand, he kept it still. Finally, he sniffed the hand then began licking it. When Envy and Yolonda came back they, saw Jewelz talking to the dog.

"So what's hood. You gon' have my back or nah?"

He put his paw in Jewelz's hand.

"That's what's up, tho."

"Sir, I'll get the paperwork ready for you," she said, winked at Envy, then headed for the office.

Jewelz looked over at Envy who was standing in his best D-Boy stance with his pinky nail in his teeth.

"Monster Don!"

Chapter 6

Dream Dior, or at least that was the name used on her Only Fans account, sat snug and comfortable against the ostrich skin seat, high out her mind on ecstasy. Throughout her body there was an eruption of an electrifying sensation that was both stimulating and intoxicating all at the same time. This euphoric feeling had her two clouds past the famed nine, and still rising.

Looking out the window, she smiled big at all the beautiful buildings lined up along Sunset Blvd. She had been born and raised here—seen them every time she came downtown. However, they never looked as beautiful as they did at this very moment.

At the young age of twenty-one Dream took pride in being in tune with her inner self. She was at one with her psyche. That's how she knew that her seeing the beauty in everything today was the result from the high off the ecstasy she was on. It made everything just hit so different. She was just grateful that she had not ingested any real drugs. This was one day that she wanted to remember for the rest of her life.

The ecstasy that she was on didn't come in the form of a pill. It wasn't even a narcotic. The ecstasy she was on come in the form of a man. His name was Rasheed Muhammed, the African prince from Morocco.

Being as pretty as she was—along with having a stacked body she proudly paid for—Dream had her share of local ballers and semi-pro athletes. But now, she had finally caught her "Big Fish."

Nah . . . she caught the Megalodon.

And just being in his presence had her in a magical state of ecstasy.

But it was ridin' through downtown Miami in the passenger seat of his brand-new Maserati that had her floatin' in a whole different kinda high.

"So umm . . . what made you contact me today after a full year of me tryin' to get at you?" she asked, one eyebrow raised.

"Finally had the time. Been busy."

"Busy? For a whole year?"

"Yeah."

She knew he was a very important man and all—but nobody was *that* busy for a whole year.

"So umm . . . where we goin' at? We gon' out to eat or somethin'?"

He looked over at her.

She was definitely a pretty girl—except them bloated Botox lips. Her titties were sittin' damn near on her chin, and the dress was so tight, he didn't understand how the thin-ass material held it all together.

But the *worst* part?

Them too-small shoes, with her toes hangin' out over the front like they was tryin' to escape.

Nah . . . he wasn't takin' her to no restaurant. Hell, he wasn't tryin' to be seen with her *anywhere*.

She was in his car for one reason—and one reason only.

"Nah. We ain't goin' to no restaurants."

"So where we goin'? A party or somethin'? The movies?"

"Nah. We just gon' ride around for a bit."

That was not the response she was hopin' to hear.

"What you mean, ride around?"

She'd been in the car all of five minutes, and already he was losin' patience.

"Look, Dream, right? That's your name?"

She nodded.

"I hit you up 'cause I seen you on your OnlyFans shit . . . doin' your do. So . . . you suck dick, right?"

Her head snapped back in outrage.

"What?!"

"You suck dick, right? I mean, them videos fire."

"In the videos, I'm suckin' on bananas! I'm appalled you asked me that!"

Rasheed couldn't help but laugh.

"You ain't appalled. You a bitch that like suckin' dick," he told her, unbuckling his pants. "Tryouts are in session. Now how you gon' act?"

For a second, Dream just sat there, mouth open, lookin' at him.

She couldn't believe it. Never in her life had she been talked to with such venom.

He was really tryin' her like a two-dollar whore.

"Look, you got me fucked up! You talkin' like . . ."

"Like I seen your videos. You on there sellin' sex, right? I'm just tryna see if you the real deal or nah."

"You think you can pay me to suck your dick? What kind of girl you think I am?"

This time, *his* head snapped back in disbelief.

"I ain't say shit about pay. Matter fact—" he pulled the car over to the curb— "get the fuck out."

Just like that, Dream's hands began to tremble.

She'd waited a whole year for this man to call her. She just knew he was gonna be her ticket to bigger and better things.

Now she was blowin' it, tryna act better than she really was.

"Rasheed, if we go to your house or get a room in a hotel or somethin', then yes . . . maybe I can suck—"

"GET. THE. FUCK. OUT!" he barked.

Dream wanted him because in her eyes, he *was* the man. He had money and power. Wherever he went in Miami, he showed up and showed out.

To her, he was *the* man.

What she didn't know was that Rasheed was only a man by age—twenty-six. That's where it started and ended.

At twenty-six, he still thought like a damn kid. Spoiled. Self-centered. Believed everything was supposed to go his way.

Hot-headed, impulsive, and petty as hell—especially when it came to women.

But none of that mattered to Dream. Not in that moment.

She just didn't want to lose her shot.

"Okay, come on . . ." she said, leanin' over and puttin' her face in his lap, hands fumblin' to free his boxers.

With everything in her, she dug for gold . . . until she felt something cold press against her forehead.

When she looked up, she got the sight of her life.

In his left hand, Rasheed held a blue-steel .44 Bulldog—pointin' dead at her face.

"I'ma tell you one more time. Get the fu—"

He didn't even have to finish. She flung the door open and took off down the sidewalk, toes scrapin' the concrete.

"Stupid bitch."

As soon as he peeled off from the curb, his phone rang. Patching through the Bluetooth, he saw *Mustafa's* name flash across the dash. He hit a button on the steering wheel.

"Hey there, old man! What's goin' on?"

"Rasheed, where are you?" Mustafa's voice boomed through the car.

"I'm over here on Sunset droppin' off this fake-ass Kim K bitch. What you need?"

"Your uncle is summoning you."

Rasheed sucked his teeth. He wasn't in the mood for no lecture or chess game today.

He'd just lost his fun for the night, and was tryna hit the club to make up for it.

"Just tell him I'll be there tonight. I got some stuff just came up."

"No, Rasheed. Hassan wants to see you *today*."

"Damn it, man!" he snapped, slappin' the steering wheel. "Aight. Tell him I'm on the way."

***

North Bay Road—aka the Park Avenue of Miami Beach.

If you were *somebody* in Miami, this was where the elite lived. And for Hassan Muhammad, this was where he had two beautiful mansions built—*from the ground up*. If it wasn't for family gatherings, Rasheed barely came to his uncle's house. With his many clashes with the feds, Hassan never discussed business here.

Even though he had both homes swept twice a week for surveillance and bugs, he still didn't trust it.

That's what Shawtown was for.

Rasheed pulled his Nile Blue Maserati to a screeching halt in front of the security station.

A tall, solidly built man stepped out—green army fatigues, Kevlar vest, M-16 in hand, and a green beret on his head.

He walked right up to the driver's side window. With eagle-eye precision, his gaze traveled *slowly* across the hood, roof, trunk, then back to Rasheed.

Then, without warning, his serious face cracked into a smile.

"When you get?" he asked.

Super proud of himself, Rasheed ran his hand across the dashboard.

"'Bout two hours ago. You like?"

"Yes. Very nice."

71

"'Preciate it, 'preciate it. Hey . . . where the old man at? He summon me," Rasheed said sarcastically.

"Him inside," the guard nodded toward the ten-foot iron gate in front of the car.

"Tell him I'm here and on my way back, would you?"

As the man turned back to the station, Rasheed looked left—five more men dressed identical to the first, lined up like statues.

Turned right—same thing.

These were his uncle's Moroccan Militia.

And Rasheed knew they'd die behind Hassan if need be.

A loud buzzing sounded as the heavy-duty gate began to open.

Being impatient as hell, Rasheed revved the engine, showin' off for the guards.

As soon as the gate cracked open just enough, he let off the brake and floored it—shooting through the opening and damn near knockin' off his side mirrors.

After speeding down the quarter-mile pathway, he had to decelerate the Maserati before pulling into the semi-circle driveway. Parking the car, he got out, made his way up the ivory steps, and rang the doorbell.

A second or two went by before the door opened—putting him face to face with *the Beast*.

Dark as night, big as a silverback, and mean as a rattlesnake, the Beast stood there with a barrel chest, slowly rising and falling. The only thing that moved were his eyes as they scanned Rasheed, inspecting him from head to toe.

Family or not, this man had one job and one job only.

As head of the Moroccan Militia, he was the general of Hassan's security detail. He was to protect Hassan against any and all enemies—foreign or domestic.

"What's up, Mustafa! Big Dog! OG, double OG, triple OG!" Rasheed said, horseplaying as he reached his hand out for some dap.

Without breaking his stance, Mustafa looked at Rasheed's outstretched hand with disgust . . . then back up at Rasheed.

Rasheed dropped his hand. "Damn, big homie, I'm just playin'. You need to smile or somethin'. Loosen up, my G."

The big man said nothing.

"Where my uncle at? He called for me."

"He out back," Mustafa said, jerking his thumb over his broad shoulder. Then he moved to the side to let him pass.

When Rasheed was halfway down the hallway, Mustafa just shook his head.

"This country has made him soft."

Halfway through the hall, Rasheed came to an abrupt stop as a heartwarming smile formed on his face.

Coming directly into his path was his beautiful Aunt Medina Muhammad, wearing a stunning, ankle-length Dolce & Gabbana dress that swayed in the wind with each elegant step she took.

Medina Muhammad was a different type of woman— very unique in the sense of understanding the ways of life.

Her mother had taught her early about the role of a woman. She fully understood that her husband was king of his empire and controlled great power. Yet, she also knew when to be in the background and when to step to the forefront.

And that was the reason Hassan had married her.

It took a lot of time and patience, but she finally said yes when he was thirty-six and she was twenty. And even now, with her being forty-four and him sixty, the two were very much still in love.

Hassan's brother, Abdula, and his wife, Mijah, had both died in a car accident, leaving behind a ten-year-old Rasheed and his baby sister, Nyomi.

In honor of his brother, Hassan and Medina took the children in. Together, they raised them until they were ready to be out on their own.

"Oh, Rasheed!" she smiled, reaching out and cocooning him in a warm embrace.

"Auntie Dee-Dee! Look at you . . . gorgeous as ever!"

"Why you don't come see your auntie anymore? I miss you."

"Auntie, I apologize for my rudeness for not stopping by in a while. I've been extremely busy lately," he said, kissing her hand.

"I understand. But I still want to see you from time to time. Come. Hassan is waiting for you."

***

Sitting at his huge mahogany desk, smoking one of his finest cigars, Hassan heard a single knock at the door.

"It's open."

When the door opened, he saw his wife, Medina, standing in the doorway with his nephew behind her.

"Rasheed is here."

Hassan stood from his chair as Rasheed entered the den. Medina backed out of the room, closing the door behind her.

She knew that, since it wasn't a family gathering and Rasheed was there, it had to be something important.

Rasheed came around the desk and kissed his uncle— whom he loved and respected—on both cheeks.

"Uncle, how are you?"

"I am fine. Please, sit." He pointed to a chair on the other side of the desk.

As soon as he sat, Hassan continued.

"I asked you here today because I have some very important news concerning the family business."

"Okay."

"I met with Julius Jackson and Da'Shawn Williams today."

"Who?"

"I met with Jewelz and Envy out of Atlanta today."

Rasheed smiled big and started rubbing his hands together.

"Sooo . . . you finally got them punks to come work for us, huh? I knew they'd come beggin' for our help sooner or later."

Hassan held up a hand to silence him.

"I made a deal with them."

Still confused, Rasheed watched as Hassan stood from his chair and walked over to the huge bay window that overlooked the lake in his backyard.

"From the conversation I had earlier, it seems that you let your emotions get the better of you. Seems you allowed a woman to get you out of character, and in turn . . . you interrupted another man's income. Is that correct?"

"Uncle, this bitch was talkin' like Jewelz run the world . . . so I put him in his place. No one in the southern United States is bigger than us. No one!"

With his back still turned, Hassan slowly shook his head.

"You interfered with the way this man feeds his family— not because of something *he* did . . . but because of the words of a female. Do you not see the brainlessness in that? The ignorance? The ridiculousness of it all? You've embarrassed yourself . . . and you've embarrassed the Muhammad name. So for your stupidity, I gave them kilos for 16.5."

"What? You mean he's not working for us but working with us?"

"That is correct. I want to see how they handle their business. If all goes well, I might just give them the state of Georgia."

Rasheed jumped clean out his chair.

"What are you talking about!"

Hassan turned around from his window with pure fire in his eyes. "I will not have you or no man raising their voice in my house. Is that understood!"

"Yes, Uncle," he said, hanging his head in shame," so, I guess now I have to deal with them."

"No. You will be a go-through to help Nyomi make the play."

Rasheed's eyes popped out of their sockets when he heard his baby sister's name.

"Hassan!"

"ENOUGH!" Hassan yelled slamming his hand down hard on the table." I will hear no more of this. My decision is final!"

Rasheed's jaw tightened. He could not believe that his uncle was doing this. However, he knew that he couldn't challenge Hassan's authority. Yet, there was more than one way to skin a cat he thought as he turnt towards the door.

"Oh, and Rasheed...."

He stopped with his hand on the door but did not turn to face his uncle.

"In the future, don't ever let a bitch cloud your decision again."

Back in the driveway on the inside of his nice luxurious car Rasheed's fist smashed into the steering wheel. Here he was thinking that his uncle had called for him to come over to help expand the family business, only to be told that Jewelz and his Trap Stars were being brought into the equation.

There was no way in the world he was going to go for that. The southern part of the US belong to the Muhammed family and he was going to make sure it stayed that way. He pulled out his phone and made a call from Miami to Macon, Georgia.

"Yo, what it do."

"This is Rasheed Muhammed. You ready to finally do some business and get this paper?"

"Stay ready."

After making meeting arrangement, Rasheed hung up the phone. He was not going to give Georgia up, no matter what his uncle said. It was just too much money to be made there.

"Fuck Jewelz!" he said to his empty car.

When the man on the other end hung up the phone, he was thinking the exact same thing.

"Fuck Jewelz!"

Chapter 7

When the Navigator pulled into Envy's yard, both twins stood up from their chairs on the porch. The whole time they were gone, Raven and Rain had wondered if they'd come back with the connect or not. When Jewelz got out the truck, he pulled a dog with him. When Envy got out, he pulled a huge black duffel bag. Seeing both men smiling, they already knew what it was.

After tying the dog up, everyone went into the house to get down to the get down.

"So, shit . . . how was the trip?" Rain asked.

"Already!" Envy said, handing her the bag full of bricks.

Taking it into the kitchen to prepare their world-famous Betty Crocker whip game, the twins were beyond excited. All Jewelz could do was shake his head as he pulled out his phone to call Jada.

"Hello?"

"What's hood, Pooh Bear?"

"What I tell you about that *what's hood* mess? That's how you talk to your boys in the hood, not me," she said, joking with him. "Nah, I'm just messing. You back?"

"Yeah, just got back. I'll be home in about three hours. Gotta make some shit shake first. But look, I gotta speak with you later on, too."

"Is everything okay?"

Usually, it didn't matter what Jewelz had going on—he'd always make time for Jada. He understood that no matter how much she loved him, she was the type of woman that needed a physical presence. But now, with the new connect and more product, he was about to be on his grind like never before. And that meant he wasn't gonna be home like she was used to. He wasn't sure how she was gonna take that.

"Yeah, bae, everything everything. We'll talk when I get there. Oh yeah, I got something for you, too!" she said seductively.

They said their "I love you's" and hung up.

"Hey," Rain said, coming out the kitchen. "Some bitch named Sugar called you on that little piece of shit phone you had thrown under the couch. She asking me who the fuck I am and shit! Better check her ass!"

"Damn, E, she act like y'all fucking or some shit," Jewelz said, laughing hard.

Envy gave him the middle finger.

Jewelz stood up to go outside and check on the dog. "I 'on't know why she just ain't hit me. She probably done sold out. I told her we was goin' outta town. That girl shot out," he said, walking out the door.

As soon as he was gone, Rain looked over at her cousin. "I know why she didn't hit him up—'cause you hittin' her. Y'all fucking."

Envy's head turned toward the door his friend had just walked out of.

"Girl, you don't know what you talkin' 'bout."

"Oh, she know what she talkin' 'bout, and you know what she talkin' 'bout too!" Raven said, coming out the kitchen, hands on her hips. "Don't no female call a nigga house and ask who the other female is answerin' his phone unless y'all fucking. And nigga, you *fucking* her!"

"Keep your voice down, mane. I ain't told Brah yet."

The sisters looked at each other, then turned and looked at him.

"Why can't you tell him?" they asked together in true twin fashion.

"Because, mane . . . Sugar in the game. Brah don't believe in fuckin' with a woman in the game. That shit can be ten times more lethal than tryin' to kill your opp. The love of money is bad enough . . . pussy be blindin' niggas. Shiiit, y'all know. Look how y'all set up muthafuckas! I'ma tell him, tho'. Just waitin' on the right time."

Envy paused, then exhaled heavy.

Truth is, I should've never let it go this far. One minute, it was just a little convo. The next, she was in my bed. And now? Now I'm knee-deep in betrayal.

"More power to you," Rain told him.

Thinking about what Envy just said, Raven went outside with Jewelz. She walked up on him while he was playing with the dog.

"Watch out—he ain't feelin' too many people," he warned.

When the Rottweiler saw her, he stopped playing with Jewelz and stood on alert. She put her hand out, but he growled and showed monstrous teeth. That made her jump back and snatch her hand away.

Jewelz was truly amazed. This was the first time he had ever seen her scared of anything.

"You gotta let him know you not scared of him. Give me your hand."

She put her hand in his.

"Do you trust me?"

"Jewelz, I will always trust you," she said, meaning exactly that.

Slowly, he began to move their hands toward the dog's nose. When the dog started growling again, her legs tightened, but Jewelz kept her hand steady. Before she realized it, his hand was no longer there—only hers, on the dog's nose. First, he sniffed it, then he licked it.

"Eww! That's some nasty shit," she said, wiping the drool on her jeans. "What's his name?"

"Champ."

At the sound of his name, he barked, then spun in circles, showing approval.

"I see he likes his name," she said, still wiping her hand on her jeans.

"Oh yeah, that reminds me. I got some shit for you and Rain."

When they started walking toward the truck, Champ tried to follow but was stopped short by the chain on the tree. Jewelz opened the trunk and pulled out two big Chanel bags and gave them to her.

"Jeeewelz! I knew you was gon' get us somethin'!" she said, all excited.

Pulling out the jeans, she looked at them, then started smiling.

"Find out you be stalkin' me and my sister's ass."

"Nah, I just like to see y'all with nice things, is all. Besides, you seen Jada. Her ass ain't bigger than you and Rain, but it's enough."

At the sound of Jada's name, Raven frowned.

"Are you with her 'cause she ain't in the game?"

"What? Nah, I'm with her 'cause I love her."

"So if she was in the game, you'd still be with her?"

Jewelz looked at her with a confused expression. He didn't understand where this line of questions was coming from. He closed the trunk and began walking back to the house, Raven right beside him.

"I don't want a woman in the game. I'm in the game, and that's enough danger for two people. I'on't need to be worried about what my lady doin' out here and if she safe or not. I guess I just don't want no chick that's in the streets. I'm good on that."

All Raven could do was nod as a pool formed in her eyes.

As soon as they walked back into the house, Rain ran out the kitchen, eyes big like saucers.

"Where the fuck y'all get this shit from? This the purest shit I ever seen. I done got me fifty ounces off a bird in this bitch! Coulda got more, but it's so pure, I ain't even wanna fuck it up."

After half the product was cooked up, Jewelz took off to Bankhead. Then Envy had the twins follow him to Decatur to show them who they'd be serving.

They were gettin' ready to officially make their bones as Trap Stars.

As they turned down a particular road in the neighborhood, Envy started to see familiar faces posted up and down the block. There were men on both sides of the street, smoking weed, drinking, trapping, and on the lookout for the long arm of the law.

"There go Envy!" one of the men said as Envy and the twins pulled up to a house on the right side of the street.

The Durango came to a complete stop, followed by the twins' Chevy. Raven hit a button, and the whole frame of the 6-4 dropped to the ground. They all got out and walked up on the porch where a group of men were sitting. Envy gave everyone a pound as the men sized up the twins.

"Damn, what's good, E! Where you find these bitches?" one of them asked, causing Rain to stop mid-stride and look at her sister.

"I know damn well this nigga did *not* just call me no bitch!"

"Let it go, Rain," Raven told her, making an attempt to defuse the ordeal before it became a situation. However, it was too late.

"Let it go? I wish-the-fuck-I-would!" she said, turning around and heading back toward the car. "Muthafuckas gon' learn today! Ain't but one bitch out here, and that's the bitch that's gon' be outlined in chalk! Got me fucked up!"

"Cool out, brah! That's my cousins from out West," Envy told the man, making sure all was understood.

Hearing that, the man threw his hands up in surrender. "Damn, E, my bad, man. No disrespect. I ain't know," he pleaded.

"It's love. Just don't let that shit happen again. Yo, where Napalm at?"

"He in the crib."

"A'ight, I'ma go in and holler at him right quick."

Before Envy could get inside the door, the man stopped him. "E, what's up with your people out there?"

When Envy turned around, he saw Raven and Rain at the trunk of the Impala, playing tug of war with one of their Dracos.

"No, Rain, no!"

"Get off me, Raven! I'm finna smoke that fool!"

"Put it back!"

Envy looked at the man on the porch who had called Rain a bitch. "See what you did?"

The man stood up, knocking his chair over in the process. Fear was written all over his face.

"Bro, my bad! Tell her my bad!"

Envy looked back out at his cousins. "Raven and Rain, let that shit go, man. Come on, I got somebody I want y'all to meet."

"Man, damn!" Rain sucked her teeth as she gave up fighting over the gun.

Raven put the choppa back in the trunk, and the girls walked back through the yard and up on the porch again.

"Hey, shawty, I ain't mean no disrespect. I ain't know—"

"Shut up, fool!" Rain said as they entered the house.

Napalm was sitting on the couch in jeans and no shirt, cutting up some work. He looked up and saw Envy with two women.

"What's goodie, my G! Damn, what you got here?"

Envy gave Napalm a pound, then sat in a chair across the room while the twins stood by the door.

"These my cousins, Raven and Rain. They just moved out here from Cali. They gon' be handling business with you from now on. Make sure my people good out here, mane. I mean, they can take care of theyself—just don't have 'em in no bullshit."

Napalm ran Decatur. That was his territory, and he ran it to a *T*. First look at Napalm and one could make the costly mistake of thinking he was soft because of how well-groomed he stayed. He kept his appearance in top condition. However, Napalm got his name from how he kept it *hot* whenever any issue came up dealing with him or his people. He was definitely one that'd up that fire.

After exchanging numbers, Napalm told them he'd take a kilo tomorrow.

"Call us," Raven said, walking out the door—followed by Rain, who took an extra-long look at Napalm's rock-hard abs.

Peeping the move, Napalm gave her a little smirk.

"Remember what I said, homie," Envy told him, catching him looking at the twins' asses on their way out.

After they left the house, Envy started the Durango and the twins started the 6-4. Hitting a switch, the car rose up off the pavement. Raven hit another switch, and the hydraulic system lifted them up on three wheels. When Rain waved at Napalm, who was standing in the doorway, all the men on the porch waved back. The girls fell out laughing, then followed behind Envy.

"Rain, what was that little wave 'bout?" her sister asked.

"Girl, that nigga Napalm fine as hell! You seen them pink-ass lips? I bet that nigga can eat some pussy up!"

"Bitch, you crazy!"

Rain looked over at her sister. "You gon' make me shoot yo ass," she said, laughing.

***

Rolling through Bankhead, Jewelz pulled up on his number one go-getter, Lil Money. He had to let him know they had some new work and what the move was that was gettin' ready to take place. He knew his lil' bro was always with the shits.

Getting out, Jewelz ran up on the porch and knocked on the door. After a brief moment, the door opened up to a beautiful woman standing there, smiling at him.

"Jewelz, what's up? Come on in."

"Koshi! What's hood? Where the broski at?"

"Money in the back playin' with them damn dogs. Come on, I'll take you to him."

Walking in front of him, she switched that fat ass like it was about to fall off. And while Jewelz would never disrespect his little homie like that, he had to admit—Koshi was banging.

Koshi, whose real name was Koshadora, was half Black, half Korean, with long silky black hair that stretched down to her calves. She was an ex-stripper that Money had fell hard for the first time he laid eyes on her. After throwin' grands a night on her, he eventually told her to get her things—she was coming with him. After quitting her job, she ain't looked back.

When they got out the back door, Money was sitting on top of a bumblebee Cutlass, wearing green fatigues, black Timberlands, and a white beater, throwing bones to his two pit bulls—Peaches and Cream.

"MONEY!" she yelled, turning his attention away from the dogs.

"Oh shit!" Sliding off the car, he threw his hands in the air. "'Sup, big homie!"

Eighteen-year-young Anthony Roberts—or as the streets knew him, Lil Money—was third in charge behind Jewelz and Envy. He was young in age but mature in his actions after learning from two of the best. Yet sometimes he could go off script and be a real live wire. One thing that was stamped was Lil Money's gangsta. Atlanta knew.

"What's hood? I see you finally got that Cutlass."

"Damn right! And I put them fours on that hoe!"

"I see!" Jewelz said, admiring the inch rims. "Locs done dropped!"

"Yeah, brah, Koshi takin' care of that for me."

"That's what's hood. Aye, yo, I'm gettin' ready to slide to Macon right quick. You busy?"

Money's mood changed as he looked at Jewelz. "Macon? Sup wit it? What niggas talkin' 'bout?" he asked, clutching his Smith & Wesson.

"Nah, it ain't that type party. Gotta drop some shit off to a friend and pour you a drink along the way."

When they got in the car, Jewelz began fillin' him in on the whole Miami trip and what they was gettin' ready to get themselves into.

"What's the what with the nephew, Rasheed, tho'? I thought it was up on that situation."

"Brah, I explained to Hassan that the beef was over a female—and it pissed him off. So for Rasheed's fuck-up, he gave us a sweet deal."

"Shiiit! That African muthafucka ain't dumb. He been doin' his homework. He knew you was gon' be the King of the South one day anyway."

Jewelz looked down at his crown charm and nodded in agreement.

Chapter 8

After taking a long, hot bubble bath, Sugar sat naked on her bed, moisturizing her skin. The sensation of hydrating her body after stepping out the tub was always a refreshing feeling for her. She had learned that lesson early in life from her mother. She told Sugar at the age of six, *"Don't no real man want no nasty behind woman."* And while that might've been too early to have that kind of conversation about men, that's just who her mother was—a raw, straight shooter.

In the midst of massaging shea butter onto her thighs, Sugar heard a car door close outside. Getting up to investigate, she looked out her bedroom window and immediately got aroused by the twinkle and glisten of the evening sun reflecting off jewelry.

"Jewelz . . ." she whispered and grabbed a robe.

Before he could even knock, the door swung open, showcasing Sugar in all her alluring glory. With her robe wide open, exposing all her chocolateness, it was provocative and inviting at the same time.

"Hey Jewelz, what's hood . . ." Seeing someone beside him made her jump back behind the door.

"Damn, Sugar . . . where yo' clothes?" he laughed.

"I just got out the tub," she said, visibly frustrated. "And who the fuck is that you bringin' to my house?"

"This the homie. You remember—Money."

At first, she was still showing anger, until she thought on the name.

"Money," she smiled. "Koshadora's man. Yeah, I do remember you. Y'all come on in."

"Brah, you remember Sugar?"

Money watched her chocolate, pedicured toes sink into the carpet as she walked in front of the TV and bent over, exposing the bottom half of her cheeks. He licked his lips, tasting the thought of her.

"Hell yeah, I remember," he said, watching her ass.

When she saw all eyes on her, she smiled. Sugar was what you called the ultimate attention seeker. She rejoiced in the thought of being every man's fantasy.

"Y'all excuse me for a second while I put somethin' on." She twisted up the steps.

"Damn, Big Brah . . . I know that pussy fire! You ain't hittin' that?"

Jewelz told him it wasn't like that with her. When she came back down, her jeans were so tight and hugging her ass up so right, Money just shook his head.

"Money, how's Koshi? You know we used to work together at *The Cheetah* and *Club Platinum*."

"She straight. Still bossy as hell. I'll let her know you asked about her, tho'."

"Sooo, what you got for me, Daddy?" she said, looking at Jewelz.

"Excuse me," Money cut in. "Can I use your bathroom?"

She told him it was down the hall to the left. When he disappeared, she slid on the couch beside Jewelz. Ignoring her, he reached into his bag and dropped four and a half ounces on her table.

"Sugar, listen. This some new shit. Folks definitely gon' be huntin' you down for this."

"Damn . . . she white as fuck. Where you get this from?" she asked, inspecting the dope.

"From a new connect. I'm into bigger and better things now, and I need you, shawty."

Rubbing up his thigh to his tool, she stroked it through his jeans. "I need bigger and better things too."

She was so caught up in her seduction that she didn't even notice Money standing behind them.

"Damn, Jewelz . . . I want you to come hit this pussy one time. I want that dick, baby."

"Look, I done told yo' ass 'bout that shit. That ain't gon' happen," he said, standing up to leave, just as Money stepped out from behind them.

"Goddamn it, Jewelz!" she yelled. "Money . . . no disrespect to my girl Koshi, but is somethin' wrong with me? Am I not a fly bitch? Would you not fuck me?"

Taking a step back, he looked over at Jewelz. "I mean . . . yeah, you a fly bitch. And you damn right I'd fuck you."

She looked at Jewelz and threw her arms up. But instead of answering, he told Money to come on.

"Sugar, we up."

"You up? So you just up and leavin' again?"

"Yeah, we up. And yo—E gon' be takin' care of you. So when you finish with that, hit him."

She was so mad she almost told him Envy was already hitting her. But she knew better.

About thirty minutes after Jewelz and Money left, Sugar got another knock at her door.

"So, Jewelz came back for a taste of this Sugar after all."

Except when she opened the door, it wasn't Jewelz. It was Deon and Ghost—pistols in hand. She looked at the two men, looked at their guns, then looked back at them. She didn't know what was going on, or why they were on her porch with weapons out, but she was about to find out.

"What's up?" she asked.

Instead of answering, Deon just looked at her with his meanest ice grill and clutched his pistol harder.

"Fuck you lookin' at like that, nigga!" she asked him, meeting his energy.

In his usual all-white attire, Ghost moved in between the two. "Sugar, we need to talk. Can we come in?"

"Not comin' on my porch with no muthafuckin' guns out and shit!"

Ghost looked her in the eyes.

"Calm down a little bit, baby girl. Don't forget—you in my hood."

The calm look on his face was offset by the honesty in which he spoke. Ghost was the head of Macon, as well as White Plains Projects. She knew she wasn't in Atlanta no more, so she didn't have much of a choice but to pipe down.

"Ghost, I'm just sayin'—y'all on my front porch, clutchin' and shit."

"We wanted to make sure you were here alone. I can't take no chances in my own hood."

"Ain't nobody here but me," she assured him, opening the door wide to let them in.

She was glad she'd put some clothes on, because the thought of standin' there partially naked in front of Deon's thirsty ass was upsetting her all over again.

"Sugar, I ain't gon' hold you long. Look . . . couple weeks ago, I'm out here posted with the bros, and I see this nigga Jewelz ride through. Later that same day, Deon tells me another one of them Atlanta niggas up over here. Today, I just come back, and niggas tellin' me Jewelz been back again. I don't knock how you do what you do, but this White Plains over here," he said, lifting up the "WP" charm on his chain. This our shit. Ain't no room for no Atlanta niggas runnin' back and forth through here. Now, I got a mean play in motion set up soon. It's gon' put this city on—and it's damn sho' gon' put these projects on. So I'm tryin' to find out, before the ball get to rollin' . . . who side you on?"

Sugar looked at Ghost and his little bootlickin' flunky, and it took everything in her not to wholeheartedly laugh in their faces.

She'd been in Macon for almost three years now, and these people still didn't know her. They couldn't have. Because if they did, they would know the only side Sugar would ever be on . . . was her own. Sugar was loyal to Sugar. Just like her mama taught her.

Looking Ghost dead in his face, she put on the most sincere look ever fabricated.

"Ghost, I was born in Atlanta, yes. But I stay in Macon. More important than that—I live right here in White Plains Projects. Jewelz and Envy are some dudes I know from the A that give me work to push when I'm at the clubs. I'm White Plains."

Ghost nodded, then turned to Deon. "Shawty rock with us. Like I told you, nigga. Is you happy?"

But Deon was still grilling.

"I saw you kissin' that nigga Envy . . . him grabbin' your ass!"

"Fuck you!" she snapped.

"Uh oh. You could never."

"A'ight, a'ight!" Ghost had heard enough. "You right . . . who you fuck is your business. I just wanted to check in, make sure you on the right side."

Sugar walked to her front door.

"Well, now you know," she said, opening it.

After they walked out, and after she saw Ghost's Mercedes-Benz G-Wagon pull off in a white blur, she locked up and sat on the couch. Lighting up half a blunt out the ashtray, she blew a big cloud of smoke and laughed out loud.

"I'm always on the right side. *My* side!"

After dropping Money off at his home, Jewelz went to Envy's to pick up Champ, then headed home. He stopped by a late-night Walmart to get the dog some food and ended up pulling in his driveway around 2:30 a.m. He knew he was late—but duty called.

Closing the front door, he and Champ made their way up the steps to the bedroom. Upon opening the door, Jewelz saw

Jada fast asleep on their king-size bed. As much as he hated to have this conversation, it had to be had. And tonight was just as good a night as any.

"Pooh, wake up, Bae."

Still half out of it, she reached and clicked on the miniature lamp on the nightstand beside the bed. Stealing a quick glance at the alarm clock, it read 2:41 a.m.

"Julius, it's almost three in the morning," she crooned, turning over. When her eyes landed on Champ, she damn near jumped out the bed. Her hysteria caused the dog to go up into a barking frenzy as he tried his hardest to get to her.

"Whoa, whoa!" Jewelz told him. "This is not the best first impression."

"Julius! What the fuck is that!"

"It's a dog."

"No shit! What's it doing in here?"

"He's yours. Well . . . he's mine. But . . . I got him for you, for when I'm not here."

"Take it outside," she said, pointing toward the door.

Jewelz took Champ outside and tied him up in the backyard.

"Bro, you literally just went crazy in there," he told Champ. "I'm talkin' 'bout you lost your shit in front of her. Now you gotta wait and grow on her."

After giving him food and water, Jewelz went back into the house and up to the bedroom. There, he saw Jada lying on her back with two pillows propping her up.

"Why did you go buy a dog?"

"For when I'm not here," he said again.

She rolled her eyes. "And just what does that mean?"

Jewelz looked down at his queen. Even though she had just woken up, she was still fine. Seeing her across the bed in her T-shirt and panties made him want to do some things to her. But he knew she was mad about him being late, and he didn't feel like going through it tonight.

Instead, he took off his shirt and threw it in the hamper. Next, he took both Glocks off his waist and placed them on the nightstand on his side of the bed.

Jada looked at the guns, then looked back at Jewelz.

"Julius."

"What, Jada baby? What?"

"What does that mean?"

"Let me take a shower," he said, then walked into the bathroom.

In the shower, Jewelz let the hot water beat down on his skin while his mind wandered. He thought about the connect the Trap Stars had just made. It was the one he'd been waiting on—the one to take them over the top.

Thinking about the connect made him think of Nyomi. Damn, she was bad. She was bad, confident, and paid. She pushed a Lamb truck. She had all the traits Jewelz liked in a woman. But . . . she was in the game. And that was a dealbreaker for him.

Still, none of that mattered. Because he was with Jada.

That thought took him back to the image of her lying in the bed in nothing but a T-shirt and panties. He'd been thinking of her all day and was now ready to show her exactly how much.

Turning the water off, he stepped out, dried off, and decided against putting anything on.

When he entered the room, she was still on her back, fast asleep, covers at her waist. Moving to the foot of the bed, he gripped the comforter in his hand. Then he ducked his head under the covers and snaked himself up until his lips were just centimeters away from her satin-covered pearl. With the curl of his thumb, he uncovered her hidden treasure.

Jada's eyes popped open in shock as she felt his thick tongue invade her middle. Instantly, her head sank back deep into the pillow and her pelvis rose up, assisting him in his meal. In one quick motion, she snatched the cover off his head and threw it on the floor. When she looked down, she was welcomed with the provocative sight of the top of Jewelz's head as the waves in his hair crashed repeatedly into the embankment of her ocean.

"Oh my God! Julius, yes baby!" she cried out, nails destroying his wave pattern.

After a mean tongue assault, he found her button and played a tune that only her body could groove to. And he played on that button until she was thrashing around wildly and couldn't take it anymore.

"Julius I'm finna . . . oh yes! Yes! Baby, I'm finna cum! Oh . . ." she began cumming. Hard. First her body turned stiff, then she started convulsing in his grasp.

When she finally stopped shaking, he crawled up to where he was looking directly down into her face. Her forehead was peppered with beads of sweat and she breathed heavy, yet her eyes remained closed.

"You good?"

"Umm-hmm." All she could do was nod and attempt to catch her breath.

That made him chuckle.

"You 'sho you good, Love?"

Her eyes popped open. She looked up at him. Looked into his eyes . . . then down at his lips. The same lips that had just taken her to heaven and back.

"Julius, I want you to take it! Come get it, baby. Take it!"

Jewelz raised an eyebrow.

"Take it? Oh yeah, that's what you on tonight?"

She bit her bottom lip. "Take it, baby."

He didn't need to be told again. With one hand, he flipped her onto her stomach. With that same hand, he snatched her little thong clean off her body. That caused a little sting— followed by a Jell-O jiggle of her plump butt cheeks.

Lightly laying his weight down upon her back, he let his dick slide right between her valley, head resting at her opening. With his lips at her ear, he began to whisper.

"Baby, I missed you all day," he said while directing his head to kiss up against her puckered lips from the back.

"I been thinkin' of bein' inside you . . . all day," he continued, teasing—rotating his body on hers.

"Julius . . ." she cried out, then put her right hand behind her and between them to spread it open for him. "Take it, baby!" she said, then rotated her hips back, causing her lips to suck his head right in.

"You want it, Jada?"

"Pleeeeaaase, baby!"

With that, he pushed himself deep into her from the back. Her tunnel was so hot, wet, and tight that he just paused, giving her just enough time to savor his full length. Then, just as slow and sensual as he'd driven it in, he slowly dragged it back out . . . making sure she felt every inch of him.

"Yes, Julius . . . take it."

Grinding back inside her he placed kissed on her back. Then he licked his way up to her ear again.

"You love me?"

"Yes baby! Yes, I love you," she said pushing back on him.

Finally, he caught a nice slow long-dicking rhythm that had her squirming all over.

"That's it! I want you to fuck me, Julius! Fuck me, Daddy!" In that moment she was hot and ready as she posted up on all fours.

Sinking his fingers into her hips, he plunged deeper and deeper into her abyss. He was giving her exactly what she had begged him for—fucking her good, hard, and deep. His grunts and her moans were drowned out by the emphatic clapping of her ass slapping up against his stomach.

"Bae, I . . . I'm—oh! Shiiit!"

She couldn't even get it out before she let go, cumming all over his dick. And as soon as he felt it, five more pumps and he was emptying his load deep inside her. They both crashed down on the bed—him on his back, and her lying beside him.

"Julius . . . I love you," she said, catching her breath.

"I love you, too."

"Now what's going on?"

Without telling her everything, he explained that he was in with some new people. He also explained that he wasn't gonna be home like he usually was. Things were about to change for them.

"Jada, I just need . . . I . . . I need about six months, baby," he said, drifting off to sleep.

She didn't want to agree to six months, but what was she supposed to do—argue? The last time she voiced her opinion, he gave her an ultimatum: either accept who he was or leave. She couldn't stand the thought of not having him in her life.

While he lay there lightly snoring, Jada climbed on top of him and buried her face in his chest.

"Lord, please . . . please look after him out there," she prayed, as her hot tears puddled up on his tattoos. Six months felt like forever when you loved a man who lived in the streets.

Chapter 9

A week had gone by, and things were moving well ahead of schedule. Atlanta was on. Marietta was on. Colli Park, Decatur—everybody was eating. Jewelz had even called his number one go-getter, Birdy, so she could put Augusta on the train.

Next up was Athens, Dalton, LaGrange, and Newnan. Word was out—the Trap Stars had that firework, and everybody wanted in. All them spots sat right outside the "A," so it wasn't no problem fitting them in the equation. North Georgia was locked in.

It was the Southern part that was looking like a problem. Valdosta, Columbus, Albany, and Savannah still wasn't converting over. But even that was a small issue. Sooner or later, they wasn't gon' have a choice but to fall in line. It was either that . . . or war.

Quiet as kept, what the Trap Stars didn't know was the only reason they hadn't converted was Ghost. Since he ran Macon—and Macon was considered South Georgia—he told them to chill. Said he'd make it special for them. And with all the loyal, good business Ghost had already brought their way, they trusted him.

Sitting in the living room, the twins and Envy were talking about the new weapons Jewelz had brought them. He had explained that they wouldn't be able to take their choppas everywhere they went, so he went out and bought them two twin .40-caliber Smith & Wessons—titanium tops with rubber grip bottoms. Neither of the twins was satisfied.

"I mean, it's cute and all, and I appreciate him goin' out his way and whatnot, but . . . I'd still rather have Queen over this little shit," Raven said, twirling the pistol on her finger.

"Yeah, 'cause this don't hit like Slim hit," her sister agreed, also inspecting her pistol.

"Listen, it ain't about how it hit. They pistols, mane! You know it ain't gon' hit like no rifle. Come on, now!" Envy said, getting frustrated.

Raven knocked back the last of her Bacardi lemon daiquiri, then slammed the glass down.

"Fuck youuuuuuuuu talkin' 'bout—it's definitely about how it hit! This our name on the line. This Raven and Rain. Nigga, when we hit, WE HIT!"

"And besides that—" Raven got cut off by her phone buzzing. After reading the text, she looked up at her sister. "Yo baby just hit."

Not able to hold it in, Rain started blushing hard. "Who's that—Napalm?"

"Yeah, it's Napalm. Look at you, all sprung and shit over this nigga. Anyway, he say he need half a brick."

"Welp," Rain said with a big grin on her face, "he can get it. All of it."

Raven just shook her head. "Girl, let's go."

As soon as they walked out the door, Envy grabbed his phone and called Jewelz.

"What's hood?"

"Sup mane! Doin' what it do over here. But peep—it's 'bout over. We need to take a trip, ya dig."

"Yeah, I was just tellin' Money the same shit. Lemme hit Shawty, see what's the what, and I'll get back in a few."

"A'ight, bet."

After hanging up with Envy, Jewelz hit Nyomi to set up the play.

"Yes, hello."

"What's hood, Nyomi? This Jewelz."

She smiled thinking of his face.

"Yes, I know. I was wonderin' when you were gonna call."

"Yeah, my fault it took so long. Look tho', I need to see you."

"You need to see me? You miss me already, Julius?" she asked, her voice sweet like syrup.

"You funny. Nah—on the business trip."

"Oh, okay. I gotcha. What and when?"

"Well, fifty. And I was hopin' today."

Nyomi told him she could make it happen, but he needed to meet her halfway in Tallahassee, Florida. She texted him the exact restaurant off the interstate where to pull up.

"Look, just to let you know, I'ma have my girls with me—so don't be alarmed."

"That's a bet. I'm gon' have my bros. I'll see you there."

Hanging up with her, Jewelz called Jada at her job.

"McCain's Law Firm, Olivia Thompson speaking. How may I help you today?"

"Liv, what's hood? Where my Pooh Bear at?"

Olivia wasn't just Jada's secretary; she was also her best friend since second grade. But she too loved her some Jewelz. If Jada ever slipped, friend or not, Olivia was the type to shoot her shot.

"Jewelz!" she said, getting excited, already thinking about his chocolate skin. "Jada in her office. Can I help you with somethin'? ANYTHING."

"You sho' can. You can put my Pooh Bear on the phone."

Olivia sucked her teeth.

"Whatever, nigga! Hold on." She transferred the call.

"Jada Cox speaking."

"Hey, love."

"Julius! Hey, babe. What you doin'?"

"Actually, I'm out and about right now. I'm on my way to Florida and I should be home in a couple days."

Jada looked at her phone. "A couple days? What you got goin' on? You got an out-of-town chick or somethin'? What—you outside now?"

"Out-of-town chick? Outside? Man, if you don't stop the shenanigans. I'ma be back in Atlanta tonight. I'm just makin' some plays for a while before I come home. Can you feed Champ for me?"

She told him she would, to be careful, and that she loved him.

"I love you, too. Outside . . . You need to stop watchin' all them ratchet-ass reality shows."

***

The whole ride to Florida, Envy kept telling Money about the different varieties of women Miami had to offer.

"I'm tellin' you, mane. Every ethnic group you can think of is down there. And they bodies like that!"

"Oh yeah—speakin' of bangin' ass bodies," Money said from the backseat. "Bro took me over to ol' girl Sugar's house the other day. E, shawty so thick. You shoulda seen her all over my nigga. If I wouldn't't've been there, she woulda raped my nigga, fa' sho!"

With a puzzled look, Envy glanced at Jewelz, who was laughing. "Damn, mane, you fuckin' Sugar?"

"You know damn well I ain't fuckin' that girl. Sugar been tryin' to fuck me since back when she was stayin' in the A— before she even moved to Macon. That's why I don't like goin' over there. Shawty be comin' to the door naked, grabbin' all on me and shit, playin' with herself. Shawty a bug."

All this hit Envy like a brick to the chest. This whole time, he been messin' with Sugar on the low—going behind Jewelz's back—and she was out here tryna throw the pussy at his homie. When he got back to Atlanta, he was done with her triflin' ass. For good.

As soon as Jewelz pulled into the parking lot of the restaurant, he spotted Nyomi's truck. He parked a couple spots down and called to let her know he was there.

"Yeah, I saw you when you pulled in. Step out—let me see you for a second."

Jewelz couldn't help the smile that crept across his face. He really liked the way she talked—like a woman used to gettin' her way. He stepped out the car.

Standing in the middle of the lot, Jewelz watched with intrigue as a stunning Nyomi strutted toward him. Her Gucci heeled sandals clicked against the pavement with every persuasive step. Her jeans fit like they were sewn on, showing off how perfectly her thick thighs curved into that small waist. She was jaw-dropping.

"Well, hello again, Julius," she said, eyeing him up and down.

"Nyomi, how you?"

"Damn, Yummy, that nigga fine as hell Nyomi talkin' to," said the woman in the backseat to the one in the front. "And he jeweled the fuck up, too."

"Hey, wait a minute—I know him!" the one in front said, stepping out the car, followed by her sister in the back.

Nyomi's eyes followed Jewelz's as he looked past her.

"Oh, these are my friends—Yummy and her sister Jaz'men. Ladies, this is Julius from Atlanta."

"Yeah, we met before. Well . . . sorta," Yummy said, causing Jewelz to squint at her.

"Oh! You have?" Nyomi asked, noticing the look on his face.

"Yeah. You the guy that like to talk to animals."

As soon as the words dropped, he instantly remembered.

"Yeah . . . you sold me Champ!"

"That's right, where your friend at? He owe me a date."

"Brah in the car," Jewelz said, pointing over his shoulder.

"I'll be damn! That's the chick from the pet store I was tellin' you about," Envy told Money, who was frozen, mouth wide open. "What the hell wrong with you?"

Money pointed out toward Jewelz and the three women. "Is that Rihanna? This nigga Jewelz know Rihanna!"

Envy erupted in laughter. "Come on, my G."

When they pulled up, Jewelz introduced the fellas, and everybody hit it off instantly. Yummy got on Envy about him supposed to have been taken her out. She played mad. He gave her that crooked smile and told her, "What better day than today?"

Jaz'men and Money were on each other from the jump. She had a thing for men with clean locs and that bad-boy attitude. And he liked her tiny frame, the little juicy booty, and that short spiky hairstyle reminding him of Teyana Taylor.

They all went inside and found a nice corner table in the back.

"Where you from, Jaz'men?" Money asked, tryna get better acquainted.

"I'm from Houston, but I been out here in Miami for the last six months. I came to visit my sister Yummy for the summer and fell in love with the beaches. Got me a job at the beauty salon and ain't looked back."

Before Jewelz and Nyomi could get deep into their convo, a long-legged, blue-eyed, blonde-haired waitress walked up to the table and asked if they were ready to order. After glancing over the menus, one by one, they placed their orders.

"Alrighty, give me a few minutes and I'll be back with your food. And if you need anything else, just let me know and I'll be happy to oblige," she said to the table—but her eyes were locked on Jewelz.

"Oh no, he good," Nyomi said, eyeing the lady.

The waitress gave a half smile, then stormed off to the back. Noticing the tension, Jewelz switched the subject.

"How's the family?"

"Hassan's fine, and Rasheed out on one of his little escapades as usual. But Hassan said he needs to see you next month."

"Let me know—I'll be there."

"And you as well, Envy," she added, and he nodded.

She looked over at Money, who was just staring at her. "What's wrong?"

"Anybody ever told you you look just like Rihanna?"

As the whole table burst out laughing, Nyomi just shook her head.

An hour later, after everyone was good and full, it was time for the two parties to go their separate ways.

"Can I see you for a minute, please?" Jaz'men said to Money, grabbing his hand.

"Lil Mama, you can see me for longer than a minute if you want to."

"And Envy, I need to see you as well, Mr. Man," Yummy said, giving him a sly grin.

The four of them headed to the parking lot, leaving Jewelz and Nyomi alone. Picking up the bill, the two made their way to the front register—where the same waitress was posted up. Hands on her hips, her smile slid from friendly to seductive.

"Well, hello there again, sexy," she said, completely ignoring Nyomi's presence.

Instead of responding, he just pulled out a stack of blue faces. Peeling off three hundreds, he handed them to her. "Keep the change."

"Thank you, sexy," she purred, sliding the money into her bra. "Will you be coming back to our fine establishment soon?"

Nyomi and Jewelz weren't a couple, but the waitress didn't know that. Jewelz didn't like how disrespectful she was being. Deciding to have some fun, he slid his arm around Nyomi's waist, catching her off guard.

"I'on know. Baby, what you think—are we comin' back to this fine establishment anytime soon?"

Playing along, Nyomi smiled at the waitress—but couldn't believe Jewelz was using her to make a point.

Okay, two can play that game, she thought.

Locking her hands behind his neck, she rose up on her tiptoes, bringing them face to face. The next thing Jewelz knew, her tongue was sliding between his lips, introducing itself to the inside of his mouth.

With everything in him, he wanted to pull back . . . but his own tongue betrayed him, joining hers in a forbidden dance.

When she broke the kiss, Nyomi leaned back slowly, ran her tongue across his lips, and looked at a very stunned Jewelz. Then she turned to the waitress, whose face now looked like she'd just sucked a lemon.

Nyomi smiled. "Nah, Bae, we won't be comin' back. I don't like how that steak taste in your mouth."

The waitress rolled her eyes and stomped off.

Outside, they spotted Jaz'men and Money exchanging numbers. Near the car, Yummy had Envy in a strong embrace—kissing him down.

"Oh my God!" Nyomi covered her mouth. "She don't know where that man mouth been."

Jewelz looked over at her. "And you don't know where my mouth been."

"Sure I do—on your girlfriend," she laughed. "Julius, I usually don't do stuff like that. It's just, she'd been disrespectful the whole time. She didn't know if we were a couple or not. Then when you put your arm around me and called me baby, I had to make it look convincing. I apologize if I offended you."

He nodded to himself. He had started it—and the waitress was definitely outta line.

"Nah, you didn't offend me. I should've handled it differently."

She stopped walking. "Handle it differently? Did you not like my kiss?"

"It's not that I didn't like it, but . . . I got a girlfriend, Nyomi. We been together since we were kids, and I'm faithful to her. I'm just sayin', I should've thought before I acted. You a beautiful woman, and if I wasn't in a relationship, I'd wanna kiss you again. Right here and right now."

When they got back to their cars, he watched her slide into her truck. He went to his trunk, pulled out a duffel full of money, then walked over and climbed into her passenger seat.

"Here's eight hundred twenty-five grand," he said, passing her the bag.

"Okay. As soon as I leave out the lot, Mustafa gon' pull up and give you the fifty kilos."

"How long we gotta wait for him?"

"Just ten, fifteen seconds—he parked about four rows over."

Jewelz turned around in his seat and immediately spotted the Yukon.

"Damn! How long he been here?"

"Oh, he's been here since this morning. He ain't gon' let me go nowhere without doin' a full sweep first. Duh."

Jewelz climbed out her truck, a little agitated. He couldn't believe he missed Mustafa's truck when he pulled in. He'd been so focused on Nyomi—and the re-up—that he wasn't paying attention. That could never happen again.

He went back to his car while the sisters got in with Nyomi. Pulling out the parking spot, Nyomi rolled up in front of the three men.

"Y'all drive safe—and hope to see you soon."

"You drive safe too."

She looked at Jewelz for a moment, then slid on her Versace shades. Turning her radio up, the speakers knocked:

—How she only twenty-one and she a savage / My bitch so bad she make my other bitch look average / I'm talkin' nasty, I call her my lil' bad bitch / She call me Daddy, but I am not her daddy—

Lifting her shades, she winked at him, then mashed the gas. The Lamborghini truck peeled out the lot, tires squealing. Both Envy and Money watched her drive off.

"Damn, mane," Envy said. "Shawty get active."

"Yeah, big homie," Money added with a smirk. "Ri-Ri comin'!"

***

Hours later, they finally pulled up in Envy's yard. While Jewelz, Money, and the twins were all on their phones letting their clientele know they were back up, Envy was in his room on his phone with someone else.

"Hello."

"Sug', mane? Where you at?"

"Hey, Daddy!" Sugar screamed. "I'm in your neck of the woods tonight. I'm in the A—at Magic City! You comin' by or nah?"

"Nah, I got some business to handle. But I definitely need to see you tomorrow."

"Aww, E, come on! I get off at three. We can duck off, get a room at the 'W'. I'm tryna get dicked down tonight. Mmmmmm!"

It took everything in him not to curse her ass out right then and there, but he wanted to see her face when he asked her about Jewelz.

"Nah, I'll get at you tomorrow."

She sucked her teeth. "Alright. I'll see you tomorrow, Bae."

Instead of answering, he just hung up—leaving Sugar standing there, staring at her phone.

***

Macon, Georgia — The Next Day
In the southern part of the state, Rasheed and Ghost finally met up to discuss their plans. Over lunch, Rasheed told Ghost he'd give him kilos for twenty grand apiece. That was thirty-five hundred more than Jewelz was paying—but Ghost didn't know, nor did he care. He really didn't even like Rasheed. He knew the dude was a slimeball, but he wanted the connect.

To show "good faith," Rasheed fronted Ghost thirty bricks—to put Macon on and take over Savannah and Columbus. Now, everything was in motion. Ghost got what he needed to feed his people and eat, and Rasheed had his hands back in Georgia without his uncle ever knowing.

***

White Plains — The Next Day
"What you mean, I ain't shit?"
When Sugar saw Envy's Durango pull up, she was excited and happy to see him. All she could think about was his money, his dick, and his dope. Just the thought of him made her pussy jump. But now, they stood in the middle of her yard, arguing loud enough for the whole block to hear.

"All the dope niggas been givin' you, and you tryna play us!"

"Fuck is you talkin' about?"

"My nigga Money told me how you was all over Jewelz's dick and shit. Then Brah tell me you been tryna fuck," he said, venom in his voice.

Sugar put her hands on her hips. "So fuckin' what, E! You think I didn't know you been fuckin' my girl Candy over at Cheetah? She been told me y'all fuckin'!"

At that, Envy laughed. "Jewelz my brother. Y'all bitches just strip together. Fuck outta here!"

"Bitch? Bitch?" He had just pushed her last nerve. "Fuck you, nigga! Get the fuck out my yard with that bullshit. This White Plains over here!"

Shaking his head, Envy got in his truck and peeled off.

***

Thirty Minutes Later—

"Oh, shit! Deeper! Eat it! Eat it all!"

Doing what she did best, Sugar swirled her hips in slow, deep circles, making sure his tongue hit every inch of her. He was lying flat on his back, fingers gripping her pillow-soft cheeks as she rode his face.

"Yeah, boy . . . that's it. Put your tongue in it," she coached, grinding while his tongue went from her pussy to her asshole.

Harder and harder she rode until her climax started to rise. Reaching down, she grabbed his head and held him still, rubbing her clit against his nose.

"Here . . . here it come . . ." Then she exploded— cumming hard, her hot liquid coating his entire face, drowning him.

When it was over, she rose up off him and fell back against her pillows, breathing heavy.

"You bring what we talked about?" she asked, glancing at his glazed-over face.

"Yeah, I got it," he said, catching his breath. "Maybe next time you'll let me hit it," he added, handing her four kilos.

"Deon, I told you . . . you can eat it, but we not fuckin'. Thank you for the dope."

He wiped his mouth and laughed, still stroking himself. "Thank you for a taste of your *Sugar*."

Sugar smiled to herself. There was no way she was gon' be without. She had big dreams—dreams of pullin' in a million dollars—and nobody was gon' stop her. *No one.*

Chapter 10

BEEP—BEEP—BEEP—BEEP

Jada rolled over in the huge king-size bed. From the loud beeping sounding off, she knew that it had to be 6:45 a.m. And that meant it was time to get up and start her day. As much as she wanted to just lie right there in her warm spot, she knew she had to get up.

With her eyes closed, she stretched out her arm and hit a number of buttons until finally the annoying noise stopped. With that same arm, she reached behind her, feeling on the bed, only to feel the same thing that was there last night when she went to sleep—nothing.

Sitting up on the edge of the bed, she raked her fingers through her hair. She didn't know how much more of this she could take. In a month and a half, she had seen Jewelz all of about three times. And both times, it seemed as if he had been coming to check on Champ more than her. To make matters even worse, the three times did not even involve sex.

She went into the bathroom and turned the shower on full blast. While she brushed her teeth, she put her hand under the water to check the temperature. When it was just right, she stripped and got in.

The hot water beating off her body made her come fully awake. Squeezing her Dove body wash into her loofah, she lathered it real good, then ran it over her body. When the sponge went across her breast, touching her nipples, they instantly got hard—causing a slight moan to escape her lips. Ignoring it, she went on to wash the rest of her body. When the sponge ran between her thighs, brushing up against her womanhood, her knees got weak.

She took the rest of her shower sexually frustrated, then got out—vexed.

Driving off, Jada slipped into her clothes for work. She didn't know how, but she had to get Jewelz and sex off her mind or this was gonna be a long, long day. As soon as she opened the bedroom door, Champ burst in running up to her. Since she was feeding him now that Jewelz was away, her and the dog had got to know one another. She had fell in love with Champ and even let him stay indoors.

"Champ, get down before you rip a hole in my stockings."

As Jada hurried down the steps, Champ was in hot pursuit. Running a little late, she opted to skip breakfast, grabbing her briefcase instead and heading for the front door. However, when Champ saw what she was up to, he made it his business to block her path.

"Champ, move."

He just looked at her.

"Champ, I'm already late!"

That made him just lay down and stretch right in front of the door.

As upset as she was with Jewelz, all she could do was smile. Champ looked so cute just laying there. At least somebody wanted to spend time with her.

"If you move and be a good boy, Mama will bring you something special home."

Getting up, he started moving in circles, then moved away from the door.

"Good boy!"

She walked out the front door straight to the driveway where she paused at the empty spot beside her Lincoln Navigator. It was the spot where Jewelz's Charger usually be. Getting inside her truck, all she could do was shake her head at his agonizing absence. Throwing the gear in reverse, she headed for work.

An hour and a half later, Jada walked through the doors of McCain's Lawyer Firm just as her secretary was getting off the phone. Olivia looked at the big clock on the wall, then to Jada.

"Liv, I know, I know. You know how this traffic is on Peartree!"

"Ummm-hmmm, whatever! Talkin' 'bout traffic. You wasn't riding down Peachtree. Probably at the house ridin' on Jewelz sexy ass!"

At that comment, Jada rolled her eyes. "I wish."

"What! Wait a minute. I know it ain't trouble in paradise. Say it ain't so," she said, getting up from her desk and walking up to Jada. "Come on, spill the tea!"

"Liv, I ain't got the time right now. I'm gettin' ready to go to my office and *Sip My Tea*! We have work to do. Remember?" she said, then turned and headed toward her office.

"Yeah, whatever! You just tell Mr. Jewelz, don't make me cut his ass!"

Jada walked into her spacious office and closed the door behind her. Taking off her suit jacket, she hung it on the back of her chair, then walked over to the wall-to-wall window. From the 44th floor, the people walking around on the street looked like ants. Moving her eyes up, she took in the breathtaking view of the city of Atlanta.

As great as the view was, Jada had seen it her whole life. She was tired of this city and wanted to leave and start over. That made her think of Jewelz.

When she first met Jewelz in school, she knew they were total opposites. Her mother was a lawyer and her father was a doctor. Jewelz's mother was a drug addict, and his father was head of a small drug empire.

Time and time again, her parents would warn her of thugs like Jewelz. They only wanted the best for their princess. But little did they know, the more they tried to turn her away from bad boys, the more it burned her curiosity about them.

Where many had tried, none of them were like Jewelz. After their first conversation, she knew she would love him forever. He was so sweet, yet as gangsta as they came. He knew how to be one way when he was with his boys and be another way with her. For that, she liked him even more.

Snapping out of her trance, Jada turned away from the window and took a seat at her desk. Miserably, she allowed her eyes to roam across her desktop at the piles of papers from cases that she had yet to look at. As she was grabbing her phone to place a call, she noticed a yellow sticky note with a number on it. She called out to Olivia.

"Liv, whose number is this on my desk?"

"Um, oh shit! Yeah um, some Mr. Jones called up here. Say he caught a trafficking charge and need our best lawyer. I gave him up."

"Come on, Liv. You know I don't do drug charges. Please give him to someone else."

Jada had despised drug cases. Being that she knew the line of work that Jewelz was in, she wanted to steer clear of them just in case he ever got caught up. It would almost definitely be a conflict of interest.

"Jada, I gave him to you 'cause he asked for our best lawyer. Aaaand . . . bitch, he said he givin' twenty-five thousand, win or lose. If it's anybody I want to see get twenty-five grand, girl, it's you. My homegirl! Plus, we can use that money to go out! When the last time we went out together? Oh, I remember. Remember we went to the Compound and that nigga with no front teeth was tryna holla at you and was spittin' every time he would say a word beginnin' with 'S' and you—"

Jada had been stopped listening when Olivia said *25 thousand.* Twenty-five grand for a trafficking charge? This guy must really don't want to go to jail. Hanging up on Olivia, Jada made the call.

"Yo, who dis?" answered a deep baritone on the other end of the phone.

"Yes, this is Jada Cox, and I'm calling from the McCain Lawyer Firm. When I came in, my secretary gave me this number. I'm looking for a Mr. Jones."

"Yeah, this me. I told somebody up there I needed their best lawyer. So, by you callin', I guess that make you the best."

Jada cleared her throat before speaking. "Everyone here at McCain is extremely good at what we do. I don't know if I'm the best; however, I do put my best effort forward and my hardest to get the job done."

"Good enough for me, shawty. Check, I'm 'bout five minutes away from your firm. If you ain't too busy, I wanna pull up and discuss my charges with you."

Being that she had just made it to work and wasn't due in court until after lunch, she agreed to the meet. When Jones got off the phone, he was hoping that Jada Cox looked as good as she sound. When Jada hung up, all she was thinking about was twenty-five grand.

Olivia was bobbing her head to Pooh Shiesty's *Neighbors* on her iPad and picking at her dagger-pointing nails when she suddenly felt a presence upon her. When she looked up and saw the man standing in front of her, she instantly dropped her fingernail file and smiled, showing all her teeth—the white ones on top and the gold grill on bottom.

"Damn, Chocolate! What can I help you with today? Or any day," she flirted, pushing out her breasts.

At that, he smiled. "Yeah, I'm here to see a Mrs. Jada Cox."

She matched his voice with the one who had called earlier and knew that he was Mr. Jones.

"Let me see if she's busy." Picking up the phone, she buzzed Jada's office. "Mrs. Cox, Mr. Jones is here to see you."

Jada was fixing her hair in the mirror. She wanted to look very professional for this twenty-five grand.

"Go ahead and send him up, please."

Olivia pointed him down the hallway toward the elevators and told him which floor it was on. As soon as he was in the elevator, she buzzed Jada right back.

"Bitch, you hit the double jackpot. He got money and that nigga fine, fine. I'm talkin' baby-daddy fine. I'm talkin' so fine, ain't no hittin' it from the back. You wanna look in this nigga face every time you gettin' ready to cu—"

Jada hit the off button.

About a minute later, there was a knock at her door.

"It's open."

Turning the knob, Mr. Jones strolled right in. He stood all of six-foot, darkskin, a low brush cut with deep waves, and he could dress. He wore a crisp white Givenchy shirt with fitted sweatpants to match. The bright white showed a great contrast to just how dark he really was. But what truly mystified Jada the most was how eerily close he resembled Jewelz.

"What's up, you Mrs. Cox?" he asked, holding out his hand.

For a couple seconds, all she could do was look at him. She didn't know if this was a trick or if she was gettin' pranked or what, but she was definitely throwed off.

"Ummm . . . yes. Yes, I am," she answered finally, shaking his hand. "I suppose you are Mr. Jones."

"Yeah, that's me," he said, while taking in her figure.

She noticed him eyein' her body and felt a little uncomfortable. "Please, have a seat." As his hand slid out of hers, she felt a strange tingle run through her body.

"Okay, Mr. Jones, before we start discussing your case, I have a two-hundred-dollar consulting fee."

Smiling, showing a perfect set of pearly whites, he reached into his pocket and pulled out a stack of money. As he peeled through it, nothin' showed but blue faces. Taking out two, he tried to hand it to her, but she held up a hand.

"If you don't mind, would you leave it with my secretary on your way out?"

"Sho thing. Um, I'on mean no harm, but you sho shawty not gon' keep it?"

Jada's eyes got big. *[Oh no he didn't.]*

"No. Olivia is a lot of things. A thief is not one of them."

"I ain't mean no harm, shawty, just—"

"I know, I know. She's much! But she's my best friend. Now, before I get the police report from the D.A., tell me what happened."

Sittin' up in his chair, he began his story.

"Well, I had just come back from seein' a bi— a friend on the westside, and when I pulled onto Campbellton, blue lights came outta nowhere. When I pulled over, the cop asked me for my license and registration. I gave it to him, and he took 'em back to his car to check for warrants..."

As he continued to talk, Jada noticed his deep brown eyes and his nice lips.

[Jada, stop looking at this man. He's a hustler. You don't want him. Besides, you already have a man. Remember!]

[Oh yeah? Then where the hell is he?]

[Stop it, Jada!]

". . . told me to step out the car. I asked him was there a problem. Again, he told me to step out the car."

[Damn, his hands are big. His nails are clean and his hair freshly cut. Look at the deep wrinkles in his forehead.]

[Stop, Jada!]

"As soon as I get out, he pulled his gun and told me to put my hands on the hood. I did, and he searched me. All he got off me was nineteen grand."

"What? Nineteen grand?" she asked.

"Yeah, then he gon' ask me where I get the money from. I told him I found it. And that's when he slapped the cuffs on me."

Jada stared at him. First, she smiled. Then, not being able to control herself, she laughed.

"I'm sorry. It's . . . it's not funny, but you told him that you found it?"

For the first time since he entered her office, he noticed that Jada had beautiful hazel eyes that complimented her skin well.

[Damn, shawty fine as hell.]

"Yeah, I told him that. I mean, what could he do?"

[Are you stupid or just a smart ass with your sexy ass? Oh God. Jada, stop!]

"Mr. Jones, how old are you?"

"Twenty-six."

[Same age as me.]

"And what type of car do you drive?"

"A 2024 cocaine-white Mercedes-Benz G-Wagon."

[Did he have to say cocaine-white?]

"And where do you work?"

A slow, methodical smile appeared on his face. "I own a barbershop or two. And I have a detail shop as well."

"Mr. Jones, you got pulled over on the westside—Campbellton Rd, Zone 4. A known drug area. You are a young Black male driving a brand-new Mercedes truck. You got nineteen grand in your pocket that you *found*."

"That's right."

She shook her head. "Speaking for the police, they're going to think you are a drug dealer."

"Is that what *you* think?"

[No nigga, that's what I know!]

"I'm not here to judge you. I am speaking about the police. So, then he took you to jail. So where did the trafficking charge come in?"

He told her that after he was sat in the back of the patrol car, the officer called the K-9 unit. The dog found a quarter brick in the door panel. He was on his way to telling her that he had let someone use his truck earlier and they must've left it in there before she cut him off.

First, she explained to him about the lawyer, the client, and confidentiality. Then she explained to him about who she was as an individual.

"Honesty goes a long way with me. So, was the drugs yours?"

He sat there and studied her for a moment. In his mind, he contemplated whether or not he could trust her. Her eyes. There was something magical about them. Something that he couldn't recall ever seeing in anyone else.

"It was mine," he admitted.

"Okay." That was all she needed to hear from him. "Mr. Jones, let me inform the D.A. that I will be the one representing you. I'll get the intel that he has on you and I'll get back to you. In the meantime, please stay out of trouble."

"I will do, and thank you."

She stood up and shook his hand. "Why are you thanking me? I haven't done anything yet."

"Yeah, but . . . I just feel more confident with you in my corner."

"Is that a fact?" she smiled.

"As a matter of fact, it is," he smiled back. They looked into each other's eyes a little longer than necessary. Then Jada broke the silence.

"Well, if you excuse me, I have to go to a couple of meetings as well as speak with the District Attorney. It was a pleasure meeting you."

"The pleasure was all mine." He walked to her door then turned back around. "And please forgive me for the comment I made about your secretary. I didn't know she was your friend."

"It's fine."

As soon as he left her office, Jada plopped down in her chair and stared out the window. For the first time in her young career, she was going to do a drug case—something she said she would never do. And to make matters even worse, the man she was about to defend was not only a drug dealer, but a fine ass drug dealer that, coincidentally, looked like he could be her boyfriend's twin.

She couldn't believe that she had somewhat flirted with another man. The whole twelve years she had been with Jewelz, since she was fourteen, she had never even looked at another man. These feelings were new to her.

"Jewelz, please hurry up and come back home!" she whispered.

"Jada!"

Forgetting where she was, she had to refocus. She looked at the speaker on her desk and hit the button.

"Yeah. What's up, Liv?"

"Damn! What you do, suck that nigga dick in there or something?"

Jada stood up out her chair.

"Olivia! Why would you say that?"

"Shooot! I'm just saying, that nigga left a two-hundred-dollar consulting fee for you, then gave me two thousand dollars talkin' 'bout that's just for being her friend. I told him, shit, I been that bitch friend for a long time! I thought he was gon give me some more money, but he just smiled and walked out."

Jada just stared at the speaker.

After seeing the District Attorney, Jada made a call to Jewelz on her lunch break.

"What's going on?"

"Hey, baby!" she yelled after seeing his face pop up on FaceTime.

"Hey, Pooh. I'm with the fellas. Everything good?"

[No, everything ain't good. I miss you and I need some sex!]

"Yep, I'm good . . . Just calling to check up on you."

But she wasn't good. He knew Jada, and he could see it all over her face. He knew she missed him and was falling apart, but he needed her to be strong. A couple more months was all he needed to move wherever she wanted to move to. However, he wasn't about to give up the connect he waited his whole life for. He didn't know how he was gon' do it, but he was gon' make her happy—and himself too. At the same damn time.

"I'm good, Pooh. We on the way to get at my man. Oh, I went by and picked up Champ to take him to Envy's house with the twins. Give you a break. They gon' take him for a little while."

"Okay . . . Ummm . . . Julius, when am I going to see you?"

He knew it was coming.

"Pooh, when I get back, I'll stop by for a while. You know I can't be home when I'm grindin' like this."

"I know, but . . . I miss you, Julius."

Knowing he had his boys in the car, he didn't want to talk about it now.

"We'll talk about it later. I love you, lady."

She stared at his face on the screen. She looked at his waves, his eyes, his nose, his mouth. Oh, how she loved this man. He really had her heart . . . but she needed him more than he knew. She stared at him until tears formed in her eyes and his face got blurry.

"I love you, Julius."

Chapter 11

"Damn! This shit got to be around here somewhere," Jewelz said, turning his head left then right. "What the GPS say?"

Jewelz looked over at Envy.

"Brah, what you think I'm going by? It took me to this location. I just don't know exactly where it is."

They had been riding around the massive neighborhood for the last thirty minutes trying to find Hassan's house. The navigation system had took them there, but not to the exact spot. It didn't matter, because Jewelz was not leaving this neighborhood until he found him.

"There it is right there!" Money said from the backseat of the rental. That caused Jewelz and Envy both to turn and look where he was pointing.

"How you know that's it?"

"Because. How many people you think stay in this neighborhood got a full platoon of green berets outside they gate?"

"Gotdamn! Jewelz, look at this shit!" Envy said, pointing to the ten men standing in front of the iron gate.

When they pulled up to the security station, all ten of the men up'd their M-16s. At once, everyone in the car raised their hands, palms up, to show they posed absolutely no threat. And in that position is how they stayed until the guard came out the station and up to the driver's side window.

After checking their credentials and making a call in the back, the guard opened the gate and waved them through.

As they traveled down the long pathway, the men were amazed at all they were seeing. On both sides were huge statues of African warriors with shields and spears. They were all assembled in attack mode, like they too were protecting the boss.

Coming to a stop in front of the mansion, all three men's breath was taken from them. The magnificent structure was three stories tall and as wide as all outside. It was built with beautiful bright ivory stone that gave off a gleaming illumination against the rays of the hot Florida sun. The palace was indeed a marvelous spectacle.

Walking up the ivory steps, they didn't even have to ring the bell before the huge double doors opened right up. And right there at the entrance stood Mustafa and his menacing aura.

He looked at Money, then shifted his eyes to Envy. Last, he looked at Jewelz.

"Come," he told them, then retreated back inside.

They followed him to a spacious foyer the size of a McDonald's. There were two spiral staircases on each side that led to the second floor.

"This guy got a balcony on the *inside* of his house," Money said, not believing it.

Straight ahead was an elevator made of pure glass that would transport to upstairs. The floor had been freshly waxed, so the marble reflected them where they stood. And on the walls were beautiful life-size oil paintings of more African warriors in combat.

As they headed toward the back, Envy stopped in his tracks. His eyes fixed on a wall-to-wall aquarium where you could see straight through to the other room. But inside the aquarium, swimming around, were two baby sharks.

"Damn, mane! Now that's what's up!"

Finally, they made it all the way out the back door. The yard was the size of a soccer field. Off to the right was an

Olympic-sized swimming pool with lawn chairs posted all around it.

On one of those chairs, at a table with a huge umbrella, was Hassan Muhammad and a very stunning woman.

"Hassan, your company," Mustafa announced.

Hassan was lying on a lawn chair in a silk robe and slippers on his feet, reading the newspaper. The lady on the other side of the table had on a two-piece red bathing suit, sunglasses, and a big red hat.

"Come, please sit," Hassan instructed, pointing to more chairs.

As soon as they sat down, the lady stood up, showcasing a very mature body. Her physique reminded Jewelz of the news anchor lady, Gayle King. She wrapped a robe around herself.

"Wait a minute, Sweetie," Hassan said, stopping her. "This is Jewelz, Envy, and . . . Money, correct?"

Money nodded.

"Gentlemen, this is the reason I breathe. This is my wife, my Queen, Medina," he said, super proud.

All three men took in her flawless beauty as she turned to face them.

"Hello, gentlemen. Nice to meet you all." She looked at Jewelz and smiled. "Welcome to the family," then she excused herself so the men could discuss business.

"So, you're Money," Hassan said, looking at the young man. "Jewelz has told me all about you and your ability to get money at such a young age. I appreciate your cooperation in making this money. Any friend of Jewelz and Envy is a friend of mine."

Money nodded and shook Hassan's hand.

"Envy, how are you?"

Envy smiled, showing his new platinum grill. "Living a lot better now, thanks to you, Hassan."

"Things are only going to get better, my friend," he told Envy as he stood up.

"Jewelz," he opened his arms wide, "how are you?"

Jewelz gave him a warm embrace. "Sup, Unc! I'm good. No complaints over here."

"Unc?" Hassan asked, wrinkling up his forehead. "What is this . . . this . . . *Unc*. What is that?"

Jewelz, Envy, and Money all laughed.

"Unc. It's just short for Uncle."

That made Hassan laugh also, as he shook his head at them. "Today's youth! Always short-changing something."

As the four of them discussed business in Atlanta, the butlers kept them full of food and drinks. Envy looked around at the whole setup and just shook his head. This entire scene motivated him to keep going until he made BOSS status.

His thoughts were interrupted by the sight of Nyomi, Yummy, and Jaz'men coming out the back door.

"Uncle Hassan, have you—" her words were cut short as soon as she laid eyes on Jewelz.

"Oh! Excuse me. We came in through the west wing. I didn't know you had company."

Hassan stood and hugged the women, and everyone greeted everyone. After the greetings, Hassan asked Jewelz to join him in a walk.

The two of them walked past the pool to a small bridge that crossed a creek. On that bridge is where they stopped to talk.

"Jewelz, I have to be frank with you. Your loyalty, your honesty, and the courage that you possess all has really impressed me. I applaud you. I have seen one other man in my life possess all three of these qualities the same as you. And that, my friend, was many years ago."

Looking into Jewelz's eyes, he took a deep breath, then continued.

"Before you and my nephew had y'all's little spat, I had heard your name twice. Once when I had made a call to check in on Georgia to see who was making moves. I was told that all was good, however, there was a guy by the name of Julius Jackson who was on the rise."

"I knew sooner or later that you would come along. You see, Jewelz, I have been waiting for you to come into your own now for quite some time."

A look of confusion washed over Jewelz.

"Unk, what you talking 'bout?"

Hassan held up his hand to silence him.

"That was the *second* time that I had heard your name. The *first* time that I ever heard your name, a very good friend of mine and I were at the hospital with a woman named Janice Jackson, and she had just gave birth to a little boy."

Jewelz's chest had begun to tighten as he continued to listen.

"Me and my friend had been down here in Miami when he received the call. We got in my jet and went straight to Atlanta to be with Janice at Grady Hospital. By the time we got there, you were already born, but your mother had died. That news brought your father to his knees. I told him he had to be strong; he had a son now."

Jewelz took two uneasy steps back. If it had not been for the rails on the bridge, he would have fallen in the creek.

"D.B.E.—Dope Boyz Empire—that your father was head of, was supplied by me. When the feds arrested your father, they offered him a deal of four years and a chance to see his son grow up. All he had to do in return was give them my name. Omar looked them in they face and told them to go to hell. He's nobody's rat!"

Still, Jewelz just stood there, trying his hardest to take it all in.

"I had to give you tough talk in the beginning so you understood that I am serious and about business. But truth be told, you are already family," he said, putting his hand on Jewelz's shoulder.

All he could do was nod up and down. He was trying hard to wrap his head around all that he just heard. A couple of things immediately started to make sense. That's why Mustafa came to see him from the start. That's why Hassan gave him such a great deal on the product. And that's why Medina smiled at him, telling him *welcome to the family.*

"Does Rasheed and Nyomi know this?" he asked Hassan.

"No. Neither of them know. When the time is right, I'll explain to them. Right now, that's not important. What is important is preparing you for the future."

Jewelz smiled at that. "That's right. The future is where it's at!"

Hassan shook his head. "No, no, no, no. The *right now*— the present—that's where it's at! Listen to me very closely. Right here, right now, this present time is all that matters. Yesterday is dead and gone. Tomorrow is not promised to no man. All the time we have is the right here and the right now. It's good to know your past—it lets you know where you come from and why you're built the way you're built. On the same token, it's good to plan out a future, to see where you want to be. But make no mistake, the past gets you to now, and now prepares you for the future. So the most important part of your life is . . ."

"The right now. The today," Jewelz answered, seeing the message.

Hassan beamed with pride. "Exactly! Today is all that matters. Life is all about the decisions that we make. Yes?"

"Yes," Jewelz answered.

"Good. So let's discuss some decisions. Let's start with that good old American muscle that you be tearing up these people's streets with. You're doing big things now—you can do better. Appearance is everything. It says a lot about who you are."

"Next, you need to invest in some sort of business to have a cover for your money. Something legitimate, for sure. Tax evasion is one of the first things that the Federal Bureau of Investigation looks into. But no worries . . . that's the reason I asked you here today."

"What you mean, Unk?"

"I know you come here to pick up fifty kilos, however . . . I have some serious business to attend on a last-minute call. If you can stay here in Miami overnight, you could go back to Atlanta with a hundred kilos instead."

Jewelz's head snapped up as his eyes landed on Hassan's. "No cap?" he asked.

"What?"

Jewelz laughed at Hassan's ignorance of today's slang. "No cap—it means no lie."

"Yeah, well, I don't be telling no cap."

"Unk, just say, *no cap.*"

Hassan shook his head. "Yeah, whatever. Can you stay or no?"

"Fa' sho!"

"Okay then," he said, turning his back only to turn right back around. "One more thing. You will not be dealing with Nyomi anymore. Only me."

The statement kind of threw Jewelz. "Is there a problem?"

"No, no, my friend," Hassan went on to explain that Nyomi never wanted to sell drugs. In fact, Jewelz was her first and only customer. Those statements kind of eased Jewelz's mind about her—which made him think of his lady.

"Unk, let me call my girl right quick and tell her it's been a change of plans."

As Hassan excused himself, Jewelz pulled out his phone and *FaceTimed* Jada. He knew that she was not going to take this well, at all.

"Hey, baby!" she answered, all smiles.

"What's up, Pooh."

"Well," she said, pulling food out the oven, "I'm cooking your favorite tonight. I got some lemon-peppered steak fajitas with yellow rice."

He blew a hard breath. "Pooh . . . I'm not gonna be able to make it. Something serious came up. But check it, I'll be back tomorrow and I'll take you out. A'ight?"

She was wrapping the steak and rice inside one of the tortillas when her fingers stopped moving and her eyes lifted to the screen. "I thought you was coming home tonight."

"I know, I know. I got a situation and ummm . . ." He looked past his phone and across the yard. Nyomi's friends were talking to her, but her eyes were locked in on him. "Ummm . . . you know I'm doing this for us, right?"

Instead of answering, Jada just stared at his face on the screen.

"Pooh, did you hear me?"

"I gotta go," was all she uttered right before she cut the call.

Putting his phone back in his pocket, he did feel bad for her. He knew she was alone and upset, but at the same time, he felt like she needed to just suck it up. At least for a little while longer. Wasn't she the one stressing him about moving and a family? All that took money. He just needed a little more time.

As he walked back over to join the others, he noticed Nyomi still watching him—not even hiding her blatant, flirtatious attraction.

It's gon' be a LONG night in Dade County! he thought to himself.

With aching torment throbbing in her chest and hot, stinging tears streaming down her face, Jada threw the whole food dish across the kitchen, redecorating the white walls. This whole thing was beginning to be too much for her. Sliding down the refrigerator to the kitchen floor, she cried like a baby.

"JULIUS!" she screamed.

Chapter 12

Jewelz, Envy, and Money each checked into Hassan's King's Palace Hotel, right in the heart of South Beach. All three men got Presidential Suites on the top floor, which showcased the most amazing view of the colossal Atlantic Ocean. Medina had insisted they stay at her home, but Jewelz explained that they didn't wanna be any trouble and expressed his gratitude for the offer.

When they left Hassan's, they hit up the strip, checking out all the fashion boutiques, some jewelry stores, and of course, the beach. They tired themselves out exploring all the city had to offer. After taking their showers and changing clothes, they all met downstairs in the hotel lounge.

As soon as they entered the double doors, they immediately felt the vibe change. In this room, the lights were down low, and soft jazz filled the air. Flickering candlelight danced on top of tastefully decorated tabletops scattered throughout the room. Instead of chairs, plush leather sectional couches surrounded those tables. Against the wall, a high counter bar sat with an exotic-looking bartender refilling drinks for the people who gathered.

"Damn, mane! This shit nice," Envy observed.

"Hell yeah it is. Let's grab a spot," Jewelz agreed and led them to a table near the back.

As soon as they were seated, a waitress came and took their order. Two minutes later, she was back with their drinks and wings. Three minutes after that, they were in the middle of a conversation about the hundred bricks they were gonna receive when four women appeared at their table.

"Ladies!" Envy said, beaming.

"How y'all doing? We seen y'all when we came through the doors. Can we join y'all?" one of them asked.

Jewelz looked over to Envy, who shrugged. He then looked over to Money, who repeated the gesture. He didn't even know why he looked at them for approval. He knew they were ALWAYS game.

After all the introductions were made, the table got into heavy conversation—all except Jewelz. His mind was all over the place. He thought of Jada sitting home alone, no doubt mad at him right now. He just didn't know why she couldn't understand that he was doing this for the both of them. Yes, she was the one who wanted a family, but deep down within his soul, he did too.

However, in order for that to happen—and to leave Atlanta and start a whole new life—he had to get the money first.

Next, he thought of all that Hassan had told him earlier. Not only had Hassan known his father, but they were best friends—and he supplied him. That piece of information was a lot for Jewelz to swallow at one time. But it did make him wonder—was Hassan dealing with him on the strength of his father not snitching on him, or was he truly respecting Jewelz's grind? He didn't know, but in due time, he was going to find out.

And even as the women sat beside him talking—and him barely talking back—he thought of Nyomi. She was the true definition of gorgeous, and she made it her business to let him know she was indeed feeling him. But how could he make a move on her when he was in business with her uncle, who happened to be the "BOSS"?

Out of respect for Hassan and the "GAME," it could not happen. But even more important than that—Jada. He had never cheated on her before, and he was not about to start now.

His thoughts of Nyomi had him thinking he was tweaking. He had to blink twice. At the entrance of the double doors, his eyes had focused—not on a dream, but on realism—as Nyomi, Yummy, and Jaz'men stepped into the lounge.

Envy and Money were busy chatting it up with the ladies at the table when Envy noticed Jewelz looking at him. After years of being around each other, Envy immediately knew something was off. His eyes went on alert, scanning the room quickly and thoroughly until, lo and behold, he'd seen them too.

***

Back in Atlanta, a very frustrated Jada sat on her couch watching a movie on *Hulu*. The truth was, she was so spaced out in her thoughts that the movie was watching her. This new dynamic of her relationship consumed her mind, body, and soul collectively.

Jada knew that without a shadow of a doubt she loved Jewelz. She had loved him since they first met. But with him now absent more than he's ever been, it made her realize exactly how much she loved him.

She wanted him home. She needed him home. She just had to keep reminding herself that when this was over, they were going to move away, and he would leave the street life alone—for good.

Her thoughts were interrupted by a loud rumble in her stomach. After getting agitated earlier and throwing the food away, she hadn't eaten. Turning off the movie, she grabbed her keys and headed for the door.

Twenty minutes later, she found herself at the front register of a McDonald's, getting herself something to eat before she passed out.

"That'll be $12.95," the young girl behind the counter told her.

As Jada reached for her card to swipe, a hand came from behind her and placed a hundred-dollar bill on the counter. When she turned around, she was met with a perfect pearly white smile, a white-on-white Dior sweatsuit, and white Dior-printed Nike Huaraches.

This man was so well-kept and fine, Jada couldn't help but smile back.

"Thank you, Mr. Jones, but I got it," she said, making an attempt to slide him his money back.

He slid the money forward again. "No, no, I insist. You're going to keep me out of prison. The least I can do is pay for some McDonald's," he said, then melted her insides with yet another smile.

"Umm, will this be for here or to go?" the girl behind the counter butted in.

"To go, please."

"For here," he said behind her.

She turned to him to protest. How on earth could she—Jewelz's woman—be seen in his city, sitting down eating with another man? Involuntarily, her head began to shake, no.

"Look, I was going to call you about the case anyway. I believe I have some news that will serve us both some good."

Yeah, that's right. He is a client, she thought to herself as her feet carried her body to a table in the back of the restaurant. *He's just a client . . . Right . . .?* she tried to convince herself as she sat down.

***

"So let me get this straight . . . y'all only in town for this one night, then y'all going back home?" one of the ladies asked.

While Jewelz and Envy were busy watching Nyomi and her friends walking around the lounge, Money—who was oblivious to what was happening—answered for them.

"That's right, one night. So y'all know y'all gotta put on! Now, how y'all gon' act?" he said, showing his gold fronts.

After receiving their drinks at the bar, Yummy was about to take a sip when she spotted the fellas.

"Well, well, well, ladies. Look at what I spy," she said, pointing to the back. "Nyomi, once again your little birds around this city come correct. They told you they were here and would you look at that—they're here."

Jaz'men and Nyomi looked to the back and saw the men accompanied by four women. Seeing Jewelz surrounded by women for some reason sent a jealous tingle through Nyomi. But it was Jaz'men—when she saw one of them laughing and rubbing Money's locs—she snapped.

"Oh hell to the fucking NO! If anybody gettin' that dick tonight, it's gon' be me. Let's go!" she said, leading the charge. And before anyone knew what was going on, they were right up on the table.

When the four women looked up and saw Nyomi standing in front of the table, they were surprised to say the least. At once, all conversation came to a halt. Everyone in Miami knew who Nyomi Muhammad was. They knew she was the niece of Hassan Muhammad. And by law of the land, that made Nyomi the real Diamond Princess of Miami.

"Nyomi, what a surprise!" Jewelz said, then stood and gave her a nice warm embrace. Envy and Money looked at each other, then followed Jewelz's lead, standing and hugging Yummy and Jaz'men. All the warm embracing caused the four women in the booth to exchange looks amongst themselves.

"Julius! I didn't know that you was gonna be here. Why didn't you call me?" she asked, plopping her soft rump right down in his lap, then looking at the women in the booth.

He looked at her and chuckled. He couldn't help it. The woman was already drop-dead gorgeous, but when she played jealous it really did something to him. He couldn't help but admire her coyness.

"Well, me and the fellas were just coolin' and stepped into this place to see what was what. But it's definitely good to see you, tho'."

The lady who had rubbed on Money's locs earlier stood up. She felt super uncomfortable now that the other women had shown up.

"Sooo, I guess we'll be seeing y'all later on tonight when y'all finish."

Jaz'men looked up at the woman and laughed in her face.

"Nah, I doubt it. Matter fact, you probably ain't gotta worry about seeing this one anywhere, anytime," she boldly stated while rubbing Money's chest.

And with that declaration, the four women left the table knowing they would not hear from the Trap Stars again.

***

"So, your friend says he's going to come forward and confess that the drugs were indeed his?"

After swallowing a bite of his Big Mac, Mr. Jones nodded. "Yeah, that's right. I paid him well to take this charge. His family will be well taken care of. So if you can just tell the DA that he was driving my truck earlier that day, all should be good. I can't afford to take any charges at this moment."

Jada just looked at him across the table. "Yeah . . . I'll call him tomorrow. So I guess you don't need me to represent you anymore."

"I'on know, I just feel like with you in my corner, I can't lose."

The statement made Jada blush.

"Umm . . . Mr. Jones, I have a boyfriend."

133

"Yeah, I'm sure you do, Mrs. Cox. My apologies if I made you uncomfortable. But you a very attractive woman. Can you blame a man?"

That made Jada smile. It had been a long time since she'd been called attractive. While many people might've thought it, they definitely knew better than to say it to Jewelz's woman.

"Thank you."

In the parking lot, he walked her to her vehicle. The whole short little walk seemed like an eternity to Jada, as she kept looking around to see if anyone might see her with another man.

"I appreciate you helping me out on this little ordeal. I hope the next time that we see each other, it'll be to celebrate our victory."

"Maybe."

"I'll take that and run with it. For now, please get some rest. You have my number from your secretary, right?"

She nodded.

"Your man sho is lucky to have a woman like you, Mrs. Cox."

Again, their eyes locked.

"Drive safe," he said, then walked away.

Driving back home, all she could think of was Mr. Jones and his words . . .

[If my man so lucky to have me, why isn't he there with me?]

Then, she thought about Mr. Jones some more.

***

After talking and drinking well past midnight, everyone went upstairs from the lounge to their suites. Yummy went to Envy's room. Jaz'men went to Money's room. And in Jewelz's room . . .

—What it is hoe, what's up / Every good girl need a little thug / Every block boy need a little love / If he put it down, I'ma pick it up, up, up—

The night was warm and the air was crisp. Nyomi stood on the balcony, listening to Doechii while looking over the great city of Miami. Gazing at the zooming cars below, the tall buildings, and all the bright neon lights, she thought to herself how much she loved this city.

She also thought about the predicament that she was in at this very moment. She had everything in the world that she wanted—except a man to call her own. And now here she was, in a fine man's hotel room, admiring the city that was practically hers . . . and yet she felt lost. She knew that this man had a woman he loved very much, and she could never belong to him.

Coming from the kitchenette area with two drinks in his hands, Jewelz stopped in his tracks at the doorway leading to the balcony when he saw Nyomi leaning against the rail. The moonlight kissing her curves, the breeze tossing her hair, and that red two-piece she wore that complimented her frame—it was a sight to behold.

Why can't I get a man? she thought.

Sensing his presence behind her, she turned to see him standing there with drinks in his hands, watching her. She smiled—that smile he was learning to love.

"Is something wrong?"

He looked at her from head to toe. "No, ma'am. Everything is just right."

Walking over, he handed her the glass. The seductive way she was looking at him let him know he'd better come up with some small talk—fast.

"You thought me and my niggas was gon' freeze up at the lounge when y'all seen us with them other broads, huh?"

"Whatever do you mean?" she said, smiling.

"You know what I'm talking 'bout."

"Okay, okay. I did wanna see how y'all was going to handle it. But yeah, y'all some boss players," she said, laughing. Then all of a sudden, she turned serious. "I also felt a little jeal—"

She turned away. She was about to tell him how she truly felt, but then thought about how stupid it would've sounded, being that he wasn't her man.

He moved closer. "You felt what?"

She turned to face him. "Are you going to marry your girlfriend?"

Her question shocked her more than it did him. She couldn't believe she asked, but it was out in the open air now.

"I . . . I'on know. Why?"

Embarrassed, she walked back into the room.

"Why'd you ask that?" he said again, following behind her.

"It don't matter."

"But it does," he said, lightly touching her arm.

"Just forget it!" she snapped, snatching away from him. She put her glass down on the table, grabbed her keys, and headed for the door.

Putting his glass down, he hurried after her, catching up right as she reached the door. When she put her hand on the knob, he put his hand over hers.

"Nyomi, why did you ask me that?"

She turned around, placing her back against the door and her hand on his chest. Sliding it down, she held his crown charm between her fingers, staring at it. It was definitely a thing of beauty—just like him.

"Because, Julius Jackson . . ." she said, raising her now teary eyes to meet his. "I want to know what it's like to be with a king."

As her other hand went up and around his neck, he put his arms around her waist, and they embraced in a deep hug, with her crying against his chest.

That night, they slept in Jewelz's room—fully clothed.

Chapter 13

"Baby girl, you need anything before we head in, let me know now."

Rain looked over to her sister. "You know what we need."

"What, some more bullets?" Raven asked, switching lanes to get from behind a slow truck.

"Raven! What we didn't have last night that you kept bitching about?"

Immediately it hit her. "Zig-Zags! Hell yeah, let me pull the fuck over right now. Them 1.5 papers burn slow, but they ain't no Zig-Zags."

After pulling up to a convenience store, Raven went in while Rain sat listening to one of Kendrick Lamar's latest tracks. She was so into the music that she didn't notice when a gold Toyota Camry pulled up right behind her. Three doors opened on the Camry, and three women got out and walked right up on the Impala.

"Hey, BITCH! Fuck you doing over at Napalm's spot? He got a fucking girl!"

Instantly, Rain's head leaned back against the headrest. She was definitely NOT in the mood today.

"Please tell me that you said you want me to hit a switch."

"No, I called you a BITCH!" the woman screamed.

"Yeah . . ." Rain shook her head and took a frustrating deep breath. "That's what I thought you said."

Pulling the latch on the door, she shoved it open, hitting the woman right in the stomach, doubling her over in pain. In a rage, Rain got out and swung, hitting her target head-on and causing blood to spew into the air. Instantly, the woman grabbed her nose and collapsed to the pavement.

"OH HELL NO!" the other two women rushed Rain.

"What you mean you ain't got no Zig-Zags? Fuck type of store is this?" Raven asked the man behind the counter.

"I'm sorry, ma'am. I ran out and we haven't stocked back up yet. The truck should be here tomorrow. If you would like, you could come back—"

Out the corner of his eye, he saw some women outside fighting in the parking lot.

Seeing the man look past her caused Raven to turn around to see what he was looking at. That's when she saw her sister rolling on the ground, fighting with three women. She turned back to the man.

"Hey!" she yelled, smacking the counter. He looked at Raven.

"What—you want me to call the police?"

"No, what I want is some Zig-Zags!" she declared, clearly upset. "You know what, fuck it. Let me get the 1.5 papers. We just gotta smoke them shits, I guess."

He put the rolling papers in her bag, then looked back outside.

"Didn't you come here with that woman?" he asked, pointing to Rain.

"See, now you worried about the wrong damn thing. You in everything but a stockroom getting my damn Zig-Zags," she said, stuffing the rest of her items in the bag. "Can I have my change, please and thank you."

Frightened, he gave her the change.

***

Outside . . .

"Girl, the hell you got going on out here?" Raven laughed, seeing her sister throwing hands. She tossed the bag in the backseat, then walked around to the front of the car and sat on the hood. "You better get that girl off your back, 'cause she pulling the hell out your hair."

Rain elbowed the girl in the stomach, folding her over. She got up and kicked her in the head. As she went in for a second kick, the girl grabbed her foot and pushed her to the ground. The two of them rolled around fighting as Raven rolled around laughing on the hood.

"I thought you was an Immortal Bandit," Raven teased. "You let this bitch get you on the ground? Girl, you falling off!"

The girl with the bloody nose ran back to the Camry and grabbed a baseball bat. Sprinting toward the fight, she raised the bat high in the air—ready to swing.

That's when Raven slid off the hood, .40 cal in hand. She cocked it back, chambering a round, and pointed it right between the girl's eyes.

"Peek-a-boo," Raven sang, tossing her head to the side with a smile. "Now what you gon' do with that bat?"

The girl dropped the bat in pure disbelief, frozen in fear.

"Yeah, Shawty Doo-Wop," Raven grinned. "Let's me and you get into some real gangsta shit."

Wanting absolutely no part of that, the girl took off running across the street.

"Lame ass bitch!" Raven shouted. Then, turning around, she popped another girl in the head with the butt of her pistol. The girl collapsed to her knees. Raven swung again—across the forehead—splitting it wide open. Then she pulled her sister off the last girl.

"Baby girl, we gotta go before One Time get here."

Rain kicked the girl one last time. "Bandits, bitch!" she yelled, hopping into the passenger seat of the '64.

Raven slid into the driver's seat, about to peel off—until something caught her eye. Posted on the corner of the store was a camera pointed directly at the parking lot.

She pulled the car right up to the entrance.

"Be right back."

Pistol in hand, she marched back inside.

When the clerk saw her re-enter with the gun, his hands shot into the air. "Take the money! Just don't kill me!"

"I don't want your money. I want the footage to every camera in this bitch. Now!"

"I don't have—"

She didn't let him finish. She raised the .40 and sent a round past his ear, splintering the back wall.

"I'll be your Huckleberry," she said with a sinister smile.

Panicked, he snatched all the USBs from the monitors and handed them over. She stuffed them into her pockets, then ran toward the door. Pausing, she turned back with one final warning.

"Next time I pull up to this muthafucka, you better have some Zig-Zags too!"

He nodded frantically.

Winking, she burst out the door and into the car. She hit a couple switches—the hydraulics came alive. The Impala danced from side to side in a smooth pancake motion before finally settling, the front passenger tire suspended in the air.

And that's how the twins from Cali peeled out of the parking lot: 1964 Chevy Impala, gangsta leaning down Peachtree.

As they sped along, Raven glanced over at her sister, who was still fuming.

"Rain."

"What?" she snapped.

"Girl, your hair *fuuuucked uuuup*," Raven said, cracking up.

"Fuck you, Raven. Why the fuck you ain't help me?"

"Help you? Girl, you're an Immortal Bandit! You ain't need no help with them Bama-ass bitches. But who you think stopped homegirl from playing Aaron Judge on your scalp? Talkin' 'bout help . . ."

"Fuck you," Rain muttered, then they both shared a good, hard laugh.

"Raven?"

"Yeah, baby girl?"

"My hair fucked up for real?"

"Yes, ma'am, it is."

"Goddamn it!" she cursed, pounding the dashboard.

***

"To a sweet victory!"

Two glasses clinked, and then were raised to their lips.

"Mrs. Cox, I just wanna thank you again for your services. I'on know if I could've done this without you."

"Mr. Jones, you don't have to keep thanking me. It's my job."

The twenty-five grand you'd handed me earlier had definitely thanked me enough, Jada thought.

"Besides, if it wasn't for your friend coming forward, and me knowing the DA, I don't know if we could've pulled this off."

"Yeah, the DA told me as much. He said I better be glad I had Mrs. Cox as my lawyer. I know a winner when I see one, and you are definitely a winner."

That made her blush—again.

"But . . . I gotta admit. I am a little upset with you."

"With me?" Her brow raised. Her fork lowered.

"Yeah. You lied to me."

"Excuse me?"

"When I went to your job to thank you, I got a look at your entire staff. No one there is as lovely as you are. You told me you wasn't the best. That was a damn lie."

Her blush deepened. "You need to stop."

"No, I'm serious. You are a very beautiful woman. And I'd be less than a man if I didn't tell you that."

"Thank you."

"No . . . thank *you* for having this celebration lunch with me."

141

They ate and discussed more legal matters. Jada felt conflicted sitting across the table from a man that wasn't her man. But her man was still out in the streets.

Jewelz had come home a couple of days ago. They made strong, passionate love and talked afterward. He told her about Hassan. About his father. He told her he was getting rid of his Charger. That he wanted to invest in a business.

The next morning, when she woke up, Jewelz was gone. And in his place . . . was a single red rose.

She threw it in the trash on her way to work.

***

After exiting Cinco's Mexican Restaurant, they headed toward Mr. Jones's truck. Jada couldn't help but notice—every time she saw him, he wore white. All white. His G-Wagon? Same thing. The whole interior—carpet and all—was white.

"What's going on with white?" she asked.

"What you mean?"

"I mean, you always wear white. And your truck . . . what's up with white?"

He cracked a smile and winked at her. "It goes with my alter ego."

***

Back in her office . . .

She sat at her desk, reflecting on how fun her lunch had been. All she could do was smile.

She couldn't believe she had given Mr. Jones her number. For legal advice . . .

"Yeah right," she said aloud.

"Girl, who the hell you talking to?" Olivia asked, walking in wearing a skin-tight catsuit.

Jada stared. "Olivia! What the hell are you wearing?"

142

Strutting over to the wall, Olivia turned around, bent over, and started twerking—left cheek, right cheek, both cheeks. When she finished, she pointed at her crotch.

"Bitch, can you see my moose knuckle?"

Jada scrunched her face. "Look more like the whole damn moose!"

Olivia flipped her the finger.

"Liv . . . I gave Mr. Jones my number."

"Okay . . ."

Jada just stared at her.

Slowly, Olivia's eyes widened. "Oh shit! Jada! You checking for this nigga!"

Jada got up, closed the office door, then started pacing.

Her insides were on edge. Saying it out loud felt like the whole world might hear.

"I know, I know. Yes, I got a man and yes, I love him," she said, raking her fingers wildly through her hair. "But he ain't around no more like he used to be. And Mr. Jones . . ."

She stopped pacing and locked eyes with her best friend.

"Liv . . . the man calls me beautiful."

"And he fine," Olivia added.

"Girl! Too fine. He wants to take me out Friday night. I told him I have a man—again."

"And what he say?"

"He said he just wanna be my friend. But the way his eyes undress me? Got me messed up. And the bad thing is . . . hell, I'm undressing him too, Liiivvv!" she screamed.

Olivia had never heard Jada speak on another man before. It was always Julius this, Julius that. But now? She was tweaking.

"So what are you gonna do?" Olivia asked.

Jada looked up at the ceiling—or maybe higher.

"I don't know."

***

"Yo, I'on know about Yummy, but Jazzy get active in the bed. I had to fight my way up out that bitch," Money said to Envy as they sat on his front porch. "I'm talkin' vice grip!"

"Shit, mane, lil' one must've got it from her big sister, 'cause Yummy a beast with it. I gotta lock Lil Mama down."

Money started choking on the blunt. "Lock down? Not Mr. Playa himself. Damn, you on it like that?"

Envy grabbed the blunt. "Me and Yummy talked for a minute last night, and shawty got a good head on her shoulders. That's gon' be my lady. We gon' kick it some more next week. I'ma fly down there."

"Oh, nigga, you gettin' flew'd out?"

"Fuck you, nigga. Sup with Jazz tho'?"

"Shawty good money, but I got Koshi. Believe me, she enough for the kid. Ain't no bitch in the world like Koshadora. Jazz cool, but she ain't no Koshi."

The laughter stopped when a new Benz pulled up.

—I used to pray for times like this, to rhyme like this / So I had to grind like that to shine like this / In the matter of time I spent on some locked up shit / In the back of the paddy wagon, cuffs locked on wrist—

Smoothly, Money grabbed his rifle at the same time Envy pulled his .45.

The door opened—and Jewelz hopped out the driver's seat and ran up the porch steps.

"What's hood!"

"Damn, nigga, that's you?" Envy asked, pointing at the S65.

"That there mine. Had to change the game on these lames!"

"She fire—and the system hittin'," Money said, nodding.

Jewelz pointed a small remote at the car. The volume turned up:

—Hold up, wait a minute, y'all thought I was finished / When I bought that Aston Martin, y'all thought it was rented / Flexin' on these niggas, I'm like Popeye on his spinach—

He turned it back down.

"You hear me? We just got a hundred more bricks. We gotta flip this shit. Money, tell all your niggas out here you need 'em to embrace the block. I'm talkin' 'bout hug that muthafucka like it's they family. We got—"

He paused when he looked down and saw the rifle in Money's hand.

"Nigga, what the fuck is that?"

"Oh, this a MP15 with flash suppressor."

"What it shoot?"

Money smiled. "Two Michael Jordans."

"Damn! I got an M4 Carbine at the house—shoot the same .223. Brah, get me two of them."

They were interrupted by a smaller Benz pulling up beside Jewelz's. Out stepped Koshi.

She wore tiny booty shorts that showed off all her thick, mocha-colored thighs. A tight white tank tried—and failed—to contain her breasts. Gucci stunna shades sat on her face, and her long hair was pinned up with two chopsticks. She knew she was a diva as she walked up the porch steps.

"Hey, bae," she said, leaning over and sticking her tongue down Money's throat.

Envy couldn't help but notice her fat ass, cheeks damn near falling out the bottom of her shorts, right in his face.

"I'm tired as hell. Been shopping all damn day," she said, standing up and dropping her bags at Money's feet. "Sup, Jewelz. Sup, E."

They exchanged hugs.

"Well, I'm gone," she said, heading down the steps.

"Damn, Kosh, where yo' ass going now?"

"Underground. Oh yeah," she said, just before closing the car door, "it's something in there for you."

While she drove away, Money reached into one of the bags and pulled out a box with a dollar sign on it. Opening it, he pulled out a big platinum chain and charm.

"Damn, mane, you gon' have more bling than Jewelz soon."

"Nah, E, she just know how much I love me some—"

He stopped short, staring at the charm.

Mouth open, he looked at Jewelz and Envy.

"What, nigga?"

Money turned the charm around so they could read it. It was about the same size as Jewelz's crown. But instead of a crown, this one read:

#1 DAD

After congratulating Money on getting Koshi pregnant, Jewelz and Envy left and headed back to Envy's. When they pulled up, they saw the twins were home.

Inside, Envy spotted Rain on the couch with an ice pack on her lip.

"Fuck happened to you?"

"Nothing!" she snapped, rolling her eyes.

Before he could say another word, Raven came out the kitchen eating a sandwich.

"These Bama-ass bitches tried to jump her at the gas station—for being at Napalm's house."

Rain glared at her sister. "God, you make me sick sometimes!"

Raven blew her a kiss. "Love you too!"

"Napalm? You fuckin' Napalm?"

"Nope. Not yet, anyways."

"Fuck you mean, not yet?"

Rain stood up. "Not-the-fuck-yet! I wasn't gonna give him none. Now I'ma cum all over his face! Fuck them Bama-ass bitches—and anybody else who don't like it!" she yelled, storming down the hallway.

"OKAY! Pop your shit, then!" Raven cheered, hyping her up.

"BANDITS!"

Chapter 14

Sugar had just sat down and was ready to grab the remote to see what was on TV when her phone went off. Turning it over, she saw the picture on the screen and her whole body tingled with elation.

"Hey, Baby!"

"Sup wit it? What you got going on?'

"Nothing. I was just getting ready to find something on this TV. I miss you!"

"Miss you back. What a nigga is talking about? You still handling business on your end?"

"Yeah. Girl, these niggas a trip for real. One side mad because I tried to fuck his man. The other side mad cause I ain't fucking them, talking bout, 'what side you on'."

"And what you tell them?'

Sugar rolled her eyes at the question. "I played the part and told them I was on their side. I got it, babe!"

"Just checking."

"Well, what you need to do is come up here and check on your pussy cat, cause it's purring for you!"

"Keisha, I told you we gotta lay low until it's time to pop out. Just chill."

"I'm chilling, I'm chilling." Sugar assured while rolling her neck. "Just ready to ride that face!"

"That's what you want?"

"Girl, stop playing with me!"

They both shared a laugh then said their goodbyes. Sugar laid her head back on the couch. That was the one person on this planet that Sugar gave a fuck about. Everyone else was just pieces on the board of life.

A hard knock on the door broke Sugar's train of thought as she got off the couch and headed for the door, pistol in hand. On her porch stood Deon with a stupid ass smile on his face. Blowing a frustrated breath, she opened the door.

"What do you want, Deon?"

"Damn, it's like that?

"Straight like that."

"It won't like that when I had you cumming all on my lips."

Sugar shook her head. "I knew I shouldn't have let you eat my pussy. Bye-Bye!" She tried to close the door but he stuck his foot in the doorway. Sugar raised her pistol.

"Nigga, if you don't move your fucking foot I'ma—"

"Wait, wait, wait." He said swinging a briefcase in the air. "I come bearing gifts!"

She opened the door and let him come in. And after a whole thirty minutes of him explaining the plan, Sugar was still hesitant. She looked at the open case on the table then up to a smiling Deon.

"I'on't . . . I'on't know about this shit. I mean, there can be a lot of blowback behind this."

"Listen, our team ready. This our turf! Besides, here's twenty thousand reasons why you should."

Sugar's eyes glazed over the money in the case. "And all I have to do is that one part?"

"Yep."

She reached for the case.

"Oh yeah. One more thing."

Her hand froze in the air as she looked up at him. He reached in his pocket and threw two more bundles in the case.

"Here's an extra five bands."

"What's that for?"

Again, the smile appeared back on his face. "I just wanna eat it."

An hour later Deon backed out of Sugar's driveway feeling like King of the world. The plan was in play and everything was gonna finally come together for White Plains. That, and he had got another taste of Sugar's *Sugar*. Life was grand. He called Ghost.

"Yeah, sup?"

"Ghost, everything a go! It went just as planned."

"Bet. Check it, go pull up on Tank and Glizzy. Tell them the play and to be ready."

"Got'cha!" Deon hung up the phone and pushed his truck two blocks over where he knew the brothers would be. Both were posted on a green utility box in the middle of the projects with their weapons on full display.

The brothers were originally from Columbus but moved to Macon to join Ghost in White Plains. However, it didn't matter where they were from; their name rang bells all across the beautiful state of Georgia as Official Gun Clappers.

Even though Ghost was the head of White Plains Projects and Deon was his right-hand man, hands down, Tank and Glizzy were the enforcers of the crew. Deon pulled up and told them the play.

***

After a long, hot, tiresome day Jewelz decided to go home and take a shower and relax with Jada. He knew he hadn't been home, and also that it was getting to her. But he was so close and didn't want to mess anything up with the connect. Also, he didn't want to mess anything up with his relationship. In his mind he knew he had to do better before unwanted thoughts started popping up and taking control.

He had been totally surprised when he pulled into the driveway and Jada wasn't home. This was the time of day that she was usually home and relaxing. However, he just went in, took a hot shower, ate and decided to call Nyomi about a re-up. After their last incident, he decided against FaceTime.

"Hello, Julius," her sweet voice flowed.

"Nyomi, what's hood! How you?"

Jewelz told her that things were going well ahead of plan and to let Hassan know he would get a visit sooner rather than later. Then they made a little small talk, but he could tell something was bothering her.

"What's wrong, Nyomi?"

"Is it that obvious?"

"To an attentive man, it is."

She took a breath. "Julius, I'm sorry about the other night in Miami. I was out of line . . ."

Pulling down on her street, Jada's mind was all over the place. Not only had she went out to eat with another man, but she had been flirting, *and* gave him her number. She couldn't believe herself. Half of her had her feeling like she was on a dangerous journey and it felt exciting. The other half had her feeling like crap for what she was doing. She just kept telling herself that she missed her man and needed to see him. Then she pulled into her driveway and saw a brand-new Mercedes Benz.

"What the world?"

After getting out of her truck she walked up close to inspect the inside of the Benz. Hanging from the rear view mirror was a Cuban link with a Trap Star charm. She knew it was Jewelz. He had always had his chain hanging in his Charger and only wore his chain with the crown charm reminding everyone that he was indeed, the King.

Happy and full of joy, she opened the front door and dropped her briefcase off in the living room. Wanting to surprise him, she stealthily tiptoed through the house. When she got near the kitchen, she could hear him talking on the phone. She smiled and crept closer.

"You ain't got to do all that. Listen, Nyomi, you are a very beautiful woman . . ."

Jada's smile faded and her creeping came to an abrupt halt.

"I mean, you're everything a man can ask for in a woman. The kiss in Tallahassee had me throw'd, I ain't gon' lie . . ."

In shock, Jada's mouth slowly opened and her bottom lip began to tremble. She could not believe the words she was hearing. It was if an invisible hand had plunged deep inside her chest, grabbed hold of her heart and squeezed it like a lemon.

"But last week in Miami, when we laid in bed together . . ."

Jada's hands went to her mouth to stop the scream that was threatening its way up. The levee broke and hot tears flooded her eyes then rushed down her face. She had heard all that she needed to hear and she couldn't take no more. Slowly backing away, she got to the front door and ran to her truck feeling betrayed.

"I felt so fucked up because I have a woman that I love and I would never want her to do that to me. I would never hurt her. And even though nothing happened between you and I, it's just not right."

"I understand. I just hope we can still be friends."

"No doubt. Fa'sho!"

"Good. Well, I'ma tell Hassan what you said. Oh yeah, would you tell Money that Jaz'men said call her, please."

"Bet. Breathe easy."

After hanging up the phone, Jewelz walked into the living room and stopped. There by the front door was Jada's briefcase sitting on the floor. He didn't remember seeing it there when he came in. Walking to the front bay window he looked out hoping to see his Pooh Bear, but instead, all he saw was his brand-new Benz.

***

While sipping on his third glass of *Don Julio*, Envy smoked on a blunt and scrolled through his digital Rolodex of women, looking for somebody to get tossed up. Being that Yummy and her sister had flew to Texas to be with their family, he had to settle for a different piece of trim today. So he let his thumb be the guide as he continued to swipe pictures.

"What the fuck!"

All of a sudden, Sugar's face popped up on the screen. She was calling. For a few seconds, he just looked at the picture. Against his better judgment, he answered.

"Yeah."

"Hey 'Nolia Boy. What's up, Daddy."

"Ain't shit. What's up?"

"You miss me?"

He couldn't believe her. "The fuck you want, Sugar?"

"Come on, Daddy. Damn, I'm sorry! So what, you just gon' say fuck a bitch now?"

"Sugar, if my memory serves me correct, you were the one who said fuck me."

"Oh my God, E! Okay, I said it. That's the past. I said I'm sorry. Can we get back on track or nah?"

"Back on track . . ." He laughed. "With me, Jewelz, or the dope?"

"Nigga, don't play me."

"Ain't got to. You did a pretty good job of that yourself."

She could tell that she had indeed hurt either his pride or his ego. She knew she had to play on that. Envy was a killer, he was a dealer, and he was fine. But through it all, the one thing she understood perfectly . . . he was still a man.

"Listen, you're right. I fucked up. I'm just trying to make it right. You was nothing but good to me. I fucked up. Pull up tho', baby. Let me make it right. I miss you, Daddy."

The truth was, a piece of him missed her too. And it was that piece he was thinking with. That same piece that was straining hard against his zipper to escape.

"Let me handle some shit first, and I'll be through there."

After Sugar hung up the phone, she just sat there staring at nothing. Her mental was all over the place, yet nowhere all at the same time.

She thought about the Trap Stars. They had habitually been good to her, making sure she was always straight and in the loop. Yet, they never looked at her as their equal—like she was less than them. Oh, but she wasn't.

Then she thought of White Plains. When she moved from Atlanta to Macon, they accepted her with open arms. Even when they found out she was pushing dope for the Trap Stars. Yet even they didn't see her as an equal, never opting to pull her in and make her one of their own. She would've declined anyway, but it was the thought that mattered. They acted like they wanted her, yet she knew better.

Lastly, she thought of her baby and the plan. If there was ever a true thing called love, she had it for Baby. If ever there was a true master strategist, it was Baby. However, with Sugar loving and being loyal to herself so much, she couldn't make up her mind on if she loved Baby or Baby's plan more.

Either way, the plan must go on.

She dialed the number.

"Yo, what's good?"

"It's a go."

In the passenger seat of the white-on-white G-Wagon, Deon looked over to Ghost and smiled.

"Come, girl. Hit me back when you ready."

Nodding, Ghost stepped on the accelerator and smiled.

***

After hearing Jewelz's conversation on the phone, Jada left the house, close to a nervous breakdown, and went to the only person she could turn to.

"WHAT!" Olivia screamed, while in the process of coughing up smoke out her nose and mouth all at the same time. "Girl, say word!"

"Talking about he going to Miami for business," Jada smashed her fist into her other hand. "Damn, I can't believe I was so stupid!"

Olivia pulled on the blunt. "I tried to tell you in school that nigga wasn't shit!"

Jada looked up at her. "Liv, you tried to fuck him when we were in school. You think I don't know that?"

"That was only because I knew he had money. And that was before you and I became friends too—but I knew he wasn't shit, and you should've known too!"

For the next two hours, Jada cried about how dumb she had been to believe him. And in that same two-hour span, Olivia pumped her head with Jewelz not being shit. Jada felt so defeated. She even smoked some of the blunt that Olivia had basically forced upon her.

And once she was good and intoxicated, she pulled out her phone.

"I know damn well you not calling his sorry ass!" Olivia said, hands on her hips.

Jada smiled at her as she spoke into her phone.

"Hey, I've decided to take you up on that offer tonight, that is if you're still game."

On the other end of the phone, Mr. Jones smiled. "For you, I'm always game."

"Good. Meet me in Jonesboro at Tommy's Steakhouse at 7:30."

When she hung up, Olivia started clapping and twerking. "That's what the fuck I'm talking 'bout. Look at you, all outside and shit."

Jada downed her third glass of liquor. "Two can play this game."

***

As much as he did not want to go to her house, the Don Julio was overpowering his judgment. He had taken a shower, strapped his .45 on his waist, and was in the process of putting on his bulletproof vest when he walked in the living room and spotted his cousins.

"Where the fuck you going with that vest on?" Raven asked.

"What's up, it's smoke. Gotta go handle something right quick. I'll be back in a few."

"A'ight. Well, we gotta go pick up some money in Jonesboro, but we'll be back later."

"A'ight, I'm up." He put a shirt over his chest and walked out the door.

***

When Jada pulled into Tommy's parking lot, she immediately spotted Mr. Jones in his usual all-white attire, leaning against his all-white G-Wagon truck.

After parking, she turned her truck off and just sat in the driver's seat, both hands gripping the steering wheel, her eyes clamped shut.

What am I doing? Jada thought. *What am I doing? What the hell am I doing! Do I really wanna do this? Do I want to throw away all that I have been through? I need to turn my ass around and go check Julius! No! He made his mind up when he had sex with someone else. Julius, I can't believe you. You were my world, my everything! We were supposed to raise a fam—*

Knock-knock-knock!

Her thoughts were broken by knocking on her window. Opening her eyes, she turned her head—and Mr. Jones was standing right there.

She dropped her head in embarrassment.

"I'm sorry," she said, stepping out of the truck. "I was just . . ."

155

"It's okay. If you're not ready or having second thoughts, I completely understand."

"No, no, it just . . ."

He grabbed both her hands and ever so gently pulled her to him.

"It's no rush. I'm not going anywhere."

She looked up at his face. His eyes. His nose. His lips.

She smiled. "Let's go inside."

Inside, Tommy's was packed as usual, every table occupied. They were shown to a table off to the side, with a good view of the stage. Up there, a lady pianist was playing Alicia Keys' "Fallin'."

He had been the perfect gentleman. He pulled out the chair for her before she sat. When the waiter asked if they were ready to order, Mr. Jones motioned toward Jada for her to go first.

Halfway through the meal, he could tell something was bothering her.

"Mrs. Cox, am I boring you?"

Looking up from her plate and into his eyes, she broke down. The tears streaked down her cheeks faster than she could wipe them away.

"What is it?" he asked, grabbing hold of her hand.

She told him.

***

Hopping out his Durango, Envy clutched the gold .45 discreetly concealed in the pocket of his hoodie.

Closing the door, he let his eyes scan across the landscape of the projects, looking for anything that didn't look right. Even though he never had a problem in White Plains before—he was a project nigga himself—he knew the law of the land. All is fair when you in someone else's hood.

As soon as his foot hit the top step of the porch, the door opened up.

His eyes landed on a stark-naked Sugar, standing there with her hand resting on her hip, looking downright fuckable.

When he stepped through the threshold, she slammed the door shut and pushed him up against it.

Walking right up to him, she placed her breasts against the front of his hoodie and looked at him—eye to eye.

"You miss this pussy?" she asked, at the same time reaching out and pulling his zipper down.

Digging inside his boxers, she released his member from its restraints and into the crisp, cool air. Wrapping her hand around it, she stroked up and down while still looking into his eyes.

"Ummm-hmmm. Yeah, you miss this pussy. Yeah, you do."

Envy didn't have to say anything. His dick was speaking for him.

It was telling her that, yes, he indeed missed her pussy.

And by the way she was stroking him, she already knew.

"Aww yeah! There he go! There go my soldier standin' at attention."

Squatting down on her toes, she lifted his manhood and—with the flat of her tongue—slowly licked the underside from the scrotum all the way up to the tip.

With her tongue, over and over, she went in circles, glazing his head—all while looking up in his eyes.

Finally, closing her juicy lips around it, she pushed her head down, swallowing him all the way down her throat.

Not being able to hold his composure any longer, Envy started feeding his dick to her throat. Reaching down, he cupped the back of her head and pumped away.

To help him, she grabbed his hips and pulled him to her more and more.

"Aww fuck!" he moaned, pumping away, while a long, thick drool line stretched from her chin to the floor. That made her go even harder.

All the way up until she heard him grunting and felt him twitching. She had been around him long enough to know he was ready to erupt.

Not wanting the session to end so soon, she pulled her lips off his member with a loud *POP*.

"Yo, what the fuck!" he asked, out of breath.

Standing up to face him again, she looked into his eyes.

"Come fuck this pussy," she whispered, then turned around and walked over to her couch, bending over the armrest, ass in the air.

In two quick steps, Envy was behind her, sliding himself into her from the back.

She was so super wet, she sucked him right in to the hilt. Her tunnel was so hot and tight, he stayed glued just like that—with her juicy cheeks mashed up against his stomach.

Sugar smiled to herself. She knew he was enjoying how good her pussy felt wrapped around his dick.

She *knew* she had that *FIRE* between her legs. No man could last long inside it.

And now . . . it was time for him to fall on his sword.

Grabbing hold of the cushion on the couch, she started backing up on it—rotating her ass in circles, milking his dick.

He couldn't help but grab her waist and go drilling for oil.

He pounded her pussy just how she loved it.

"Come on, Daddy, fuck me, umm-hmm, yeah! Get it, baby. Get it!"

He started grunting and twitching.

"You ready? Huh. You ready?"

His abs and her ass hitting together was a continuous thunderclap being echoed throughout the room.

"Oooh shit . . ."

He was ready.

Quickly, she dislodged, turned around, and squatted back on her toes. Putting her lips back around his dick, she could taste her own juices on him—and that turned her out. She went for broke, hand and mouth on one accord, sucking and stroking faster and faster.

All the way up until he couldn't hold it any longer and let loose, emptying out his load. When she tasted it, she went even harder. Arching her throat, she deep-throated and worked her magic.

"Damn, I miss that shit," she said, standing up and wiping her mouth.

She went into the kitchen to fix two drinks. When she came out, Envy was putting himself back into his pants.

"Here you go," she said, attempting to hand him one of the glasses.

"Nah, mane. I gotta get back."

"WHAT! So you think you just gon' come over here, get your dick sucked, get a shot of pussy, and just walk out? We ain't even talked yet."

"Ain't shit to talk about," he said, moving toward the front door. "What's done is done. And we done."

When Envy first walked in and she laid eyes on him, she knew she missed him. His drip, his smile, talk, dick game—everything. She was having second thoughts on setting him up. But the way he was being with her at this exact moment? Hell nah.

Sugar smiled.

"You got it. But look, before you leave, can you at least go to the corner store and get me some baking soda while I get in the shower?"

He wanted to tell her no, but figured it was the least he could do. And the last.

***

"So you really gonna fuck Napalm?" Raven asked her sister between bites of her burger.

The sisters had traveled right outside Atlanta to pick up some money owed to them. Before going back to the city, they made a stop to get some food at a very popular steakhouse in Jonesboro.

"I'on know. Maybe. I mean, he fine as shit, and these other niggas is goofy. Well, Money like that, tho. But he already got his lady."

"What? Money?"

"Hell yeah," Raven doubled down. "And that nigga a gangsta. He a perfect fit with Jewelz and E. Koshi, or whatever her name is, better keep an eye on his ass."

They both laughed at that.

"Girl, you crazy as—" Rain stopped mid-sentence as a look of horror crossed her face.

"What's wrong with you?"

Rain pointed across the room to the back corner. Raven's eyes almost popped out her head when she saw Jada sitting with a man wearing all white—holding hands, looking into each other's eyes.

"What the fuck!" Raven said, standing up. "Bitch playing my nigga. I'm finna drag this bitch!"

Rain grabbed her arm. "Raven, no!"

"Fuck you mean, no? Brah love this bitch and she out here in Jonesboro thotin' around . . . fuck that!"

"Rain, what the fuck is wrong with you? Do you see this shit? Do you see it!"

"Be easy, Raven. If you beat that girl ass, Jewelz will never forgive you. For now, let it be. Not here. Not now."

"Yeah, a'ight," Raven said, snatching away from her sister's grip. "But that bitch gon' catch this fade." She pulled out her phone and snapped a picture of them.

***

"That was the call. You ready?"

Putting the clip in his nine, Glizzy blew smoke from the blunt out his nose. "Let's get this fucka," he told Tank.

The brothers went out the back door of the traphouse, which was right behind the store. Crossing the backyard, they cleared a fence and were right at their destination.

Tank pointed to the Durango. "Let's leave this nigga leaking."

They split up to take their positions.

When Envy came out the store, he saw a man leaning up against his truck. Knowing he was on foreign land, his hand automatically reached inside his hoodie pocket to clutch his pistol.

"What's up, mane!"

The man turned around to face him, and Envy saw the tank chain hanging from his necklace. He knew exactly who the man was.

"Sup, homie. This your truck?" Tank asked.

"Sho is. You mind getting your happy ass the fuck up off it?"

When Tank smiled, Envy knew what time it was. Dropping the bag, him and Tank up'd at the same time. And like that, shots started piercing the air.

One of the slugs from Envy's .45 hit Tank in the leg, causing him to drop his gun and go down.

"Fuck nigga, what—you thought this shit was sweet?" Envy said, walking up, preparing to finish him off.

That's when he heard what sounded like a cannon rapid-repelling. The loud sound of the 9 firing back-to-back made Envy look back to see where the shots were coming from. That's when he saw a man biting on his bottom lip, busting his gun.

When three shots tore into the Durango's door, just missing him, Envy dove to the other side for cover. Glizzy ran up on the truck, squeezing—keeping it hot. Knowing the attacker was close, Envy had to think fast.

Clenching his teeth, Envy stood and let his .45 ring. That made Glizzy fall for cover beside his brother. Knowing he now had two attackers on the other side of his truck, he had to get space between them. He started backpedaling toward the store, still busting his gun, holding Tank and Glizzy pinned down. When his back hit the store, he stopped shooting to turn the corner for safety.

And that cost him.

Timing it just perfect, Glizzy leaned on the hood of Envy's truck and put him in his sights. He exhaled slowly, then squeezed the trigger.

What seemed like slow motion—the hammer struck the bullet, causing the slide action to cock back and eject the spent shell casing. Then the slug came flying out the barrel, followed by a stream of fire and a loud bang.

As Envy turned the corner, the slug ripped into the back of his shoulder and exploded out the front. A sharp pain hit him as he dropped his gun. Instinctively, he grabbed his shoulder—and half his hand went inside the hole. Breathing hard, he bent down to pick up his pistol.

When he stood up, he saw a third man walking toward him smiling.

Deon.

Envy looked at the 12-gauge Mossberg pistol pointed at his chest. His left eye twitched as he wondered if he could up the .45 before Deon pulled the trigger.

It took him 0.56 seconds to find out.

Deon pulled the trigger and shot Envy right in the chest. The impact knocked him clean off his feet, sending him airborne—then back down on his back. His mouth was open in shock.

If it wasn't for the vest, he wouldn't have had a chest.

Rolling over on his side, he heard more footsteps, but the pain in his chest and shoulder hurt so bad he couldn't even get up. On all fours, he looked up and saw Glizzy and Deon standing over him. With blood leaking from his shoulder and mouth, he looked at his gun, which was about ten feet away. Then he looked back at the two goons.

Glizzy pointed the 9 right at Envy's face.

"Bitch-ass nigga. White Plains!" he said, then squeezed the trigger.

***

"I had a nice time, and I thank you for being my ear," Jada said to Mr. Jones as he walked her to her car.

"I'm glad you had a nice time. I did too. And any night of the year, I'll be your ear."

"Hey, you better watch what you say. I might just take you up on that."

They were interrupted by his phone.

"Excuse me for one second," he said, answering. "Yeah?"

"It's done. We smokin' on Trap Stars tonight, Big Homie!"

"Bet. I'll get back."

He turned his attention back to Jada, who was leaning against her Navigator, looking sexy.

"Mrs. Cox, I have to go, but please tell me when we'll do this again?"

She walked up to him and kissed him on the cheek.

"Only if you promise to call me Jada."

"Okay, Jada. But you have to call me by my name too."

"What is your name?"

He looked at her and smiled.

"Ghost."

To be continued.

Lock Down Publications and Ca$h Presents
Assisted Publishing Packages

Due to an increase in the price of services we have increased our prices. The prices below reflect the price increase as of 11/1/24.

BASIC PACKAGE	UPGRADED PACKAGE
$699	**$1000**
Editing	Typing
Cover Design	Editing
Formatting	Cover Design
	Formatting
	Upload eBooks to Amazon
	Upload Paperback to Amazon
ADVANCE PACKAGE	**LDP SUPREME PACKAGE**
$1,400	**$1,700**
Typing	Typing
Editing (line editing/content)	Editing (line editing/content)
Cover Design	Cover Design
Formatting	Formatting
Copyright Registration	Copyright Registration
Proofreading	Proofreading
Upload eBooks to Amazon	Set up Amazon Account
Upload Paperback to Amazon	Upload eBooks to Amazon
	Upload Paperback to Amazon
	Advertise on LDP's Amazon and Facebook Page

***

Other services available upon request.
Additional charges may apply

Lock Down Publications
P.O. Box 944
Stockbridge, GA 30281-9998
Phone: 470 303-9761
Email: lockdownpublications@gmail.com

Submission Guideline

Submit the first three chapters of your completed manuscript to ldpsubmissions@gmail.com. In the subject line add **Your Book's Title**. The manuscript must be in a Word Doc file and sent as an attachment. Document should be in Times New Roman, double spaced, and in size 12 font. Also, provide your synopsis and full contact information. If sending multiple submissions, they must each be in a separate email.

Have a story but no way to send it electronically? You can still submit to LDP/Ca$h Presents. Send in the first three chapters, written or typed, of your completed manuscript to:

LDP: Submissions Dept
P.O. Box 944
Stockbridge, GA 30281-9998

DO NOT send original manuscript. Must be a duplicate.
Provide your synopsis and a cover letter containing your full contact information.

Thanks for considering LDP and Ca$h Presents.

NEW RELEASES

BLOODLINE OF A SAVAGE 1-3
THESE VICIOUS STREETS 1-3
RELENTLESS GOON 1-3
BY PRINCE A. TAUHID

THE BUTTERFLY MAFIA 1-3
BY FUMIYA PAYNE

A THUG'S STREET PRINCESS 1&2
BY MEESHA

CITY OF SMOKE 3
BY MOLOTTI

GET IT IN SLUGS 1 &2
BY B. STALL

STANDING ON HER BUSINESS 1&2
BY DG SANTANA

STEPPERS 1,2&3
THE REAL BADDIES OF CHI-RAQ
BY KING RIO

THE LANE 1&2
BY KEN-KEN SPENCE

THUG OF SPADES 1&2
LOVE IN THE TRENCHES 2
CORNER BOYS
BY COREY ROBINSON

TIL DEATH 3
BY ARYANNA

TRAP STARS | B. SHELLY

THE BIRTH OF A GANGSTER 4
BY DELMONT PLAYER

PRODUCT OF THE STREETS 1-3
BY DEMOND "MONEY" ANDERSON

NO TIME FOR ERROR
BY KEESE

MONEY HUNGRY DEMONS 1-2
BY TRANAY ADAMS

HUB CITY MENACE 1-3
BY J. WHITE

A THUGGISH PASSION 1&2
LAND OF DA HOOLIGANZ 1-4
KILLAZ ON STANDBY 1&2
BY IRA B.

FO'EVA ROLLIN 1&2
BY ASSA RAYMOND BAKER

THE LEVEL UP 1&3
BY LUXURY KING

Coming Soon from Lock Down Publications/Ca$h Presents

IF YOU CROSS ME ONCE 6
ANGEL V
By Anthony Fields

A THUGS STREET PRINCESS 3
By Meesha

CORNER BOYS 2
By Corey Robinson

THA TAKEOVER
By Keith Chandler

BETRAYAL OF A G 2
By Ray Vinci

SAVAGE FAMILY EMPIRE 1&2
SOULLESS GOON 1,2&3
THE DIRTY SIDE OF MONEY 1,2&3
By Prince

FOR MY ENEMY'S SAKE
AMBITIONS OF A SLIDER
FRESH OFF DA PORCH
By IRA B.

BY THE TRUCKLOAD 1-4
TIPPIN' THE SCALES 1-3
BAD BITCHES WIT GUNZ 3
PROBLEM SOLVED 2
By Christopher "Diesel" Hornezes

Available Now

RESTRAINING ORDER 1 & 2
By **CA$H & Coffee**

LOVE KNOWS NO BOUNDARIES 1-3
By **Coffee**

RAISED AS A GOON I, II, III & IV
BRED BY THE SLUMS I, II, III
BLAST FOR ME I & II
ROTTEN TO THE CORE I II III
A BRONX TALE I, II, III
DUFFLE BAG CARTEL I II III IV V VI
HEARTLESS GOON I II III IV V
A SAVAGE DOPEBOY I II
DRUG LORDS I II III
CUTTHROAT MAFIA I II
KING OF THE TRENCHES
By **Ghost**

LAY IT DOWN I & II
LAST OF A DYING BREED I II
BLOOD STAINS OF A SHOTTA I & II III
By **Jamaica**

LOYAL TO THE GAME I II III
LIFE OF SIN I, II III
By **TJ & Jelissa**

IF LOVING HIM IS WRONG…I & II
LOVE ME EVEN WHEN IT HURTS I II III
By **Jelissa**

PUSH IT TO THE LIMIT
By **Bre' Hayes**

TRAP STARS | B. SHELLY

BLOODY COMMAS I & II
SKI MASK CARTEL I, II & III
KING OF NEW YORK I II, III IV V
RISE TO POWER I II III
COKE KINGS I II III IV V
BORN HEARTLESS I II III IV
KING OF THE TRAP I II
By **T.J. Edwards**

WHEN THE STREETS CLAP BACK I & II III
THE HEART OF A SAVAGE I II III IV
MONEY MAFIA I II
LOYAL TO THE SOIL I II III
By **Jibril Williams**

A DISTINGUISHED THUG STOLE MY HEART I II & III
LOVE SHOULDN'T HURT I II III IV
RENEGADE BOYS 1-4
PAID IN KARMA 1-3
SAVAGE STORMS 1-3
AN UNFORESEEN LOVE 1-3
BABY, I'M WINTERTIME COLD 1-3
A THUG'S STREET PRINCESS 1&2
By **Meesha**

A GANGSTER'S CODE 1-3
A GANGSTER'S SYN 1-3
THE SAVAGE LIFE 1-3
CHAINED TO THE STREETS 1-3
BLOOD ON THE MONEY 1-3
A GANGSTA'S PAIN 1-3
BEAUTIFUL LIES AND UGLY TRUTHS
CHURCH IN THESE STREETS
By **J-Blunt**

CUM FOR ME 1-8
An LDP Erotica Collaboration

TRAP STARS | B. SHELLY

BLOOD OF A BOSS 1-5
SHADOWS OF THE GAME
TRAP BASTARD
By **Askari**

THE STREETS BLEED MURDER 1-3
THE HEART OF A GANGSTA 1-3
By **Jerry Jackson**

WHEN A GOOD GIRL GOES BAD
By **Adrienne**

THE COST OF LOYALTY 1-3
By **Kweli**

BRIDE OF A HUSTLA 1-3
THE FETTI GIRLS 1-3
CORRUPTED BY A GANGSTA 1-4
BLINDED BY HIS LOVE
THE PRICE YOU PAY FOR LOVE 1-3
DOPE GIRL MAGIC 1-3
By **Destiny Skai**

A KINGPIN'S AMBITION
A KINGPIN'S AMBITION II
I MURDER FOR THE DOUGH
By **Ambitious**

TRUE SAVAGE 1-7
DOPE BOY MAGIC 1-3
MIDNIGHT CARTEL 1-3
CITY OF KINGZ 1&2
NIGHTMARE ON SILENT AVE
THE PLUG OF LIL MEXICO 1&2
CLASSIC CITY
By **Chris Green**

TRAP STARS | B. SHELLY

A GANGSTER'S REVENGE 1-4
THE BOSS MAN'S DAUGHTERS 1-5
A SAVAGE LOVE 1&2
BAE BELONGS TO ME 1&2
A HUSTLER'S DECEIT 1-3
WHAT BAD BITCHES DO 1-3
SOUL OF A MONSTER 1-3
KILL ZONE
A DOPE BOY'S QUEEN 1-3
TIL DEATH 1-3
IMMA DIE BOUT MINE 1-6
DYING FOR LIKES
By **Aryanna**

A DOPEBOY'S PRAYER
By **Eddie "Wolf" Lee**

THE KING CARTEL 1-3
By **Frank Gresham**

THESE NIGGAS AIN'T LOYAL 1-3
By **Nikki Tee**

GANGSTA SHYT 1-3
By **CATO**

THE ULTIMATE BETRAYAL
By **Phoenix**

BOSS'N UP 1-3
By **Royal Nicole**

I LOVE YOU TO DEATH
By **Destiny J**

I RIDE FOR MY HITTA
I STILL RIDE FOR MY HITTA
By **Misty Holt**

TRAP STARS | B. SHELLY

LOVE & CHASIN' PAPER
By **Qay Crockett**

TO DIE IN VAIN
SINS OF A HUSTLA
By **ASAD**

BROOKLYN HUSTLAZ
By **Boogsy Morina**

BROOKLYN ON LOCK 1 & 2
By **Sonovia**

GANGSTA CITY
By **Teddy Duke**

A DRUG KING AND HIS DIAMOND 1-3
A DOPEMAN'S RICHES
HER MAN, MINE'S TOO 1&2
CASH MONEY HO'S
THE WIFEY I USED TO BE 1&2
PRETTY GIRLS DO NASTY THINGS
By **Nicole Goosby**

LIPSTICK KILLAH 1-3
CRIME OF PASSION 1-3
FRIEND OR FOE 1-3
By **Mimi**

TRAPHOUSE KING 1-3
KINGPIN KILLAZ 1-3
STREET KINGS 1&2
PAID IN BLOOD 1&2
CARTEL KILLAZ 1-3
DOPE GODS 1&2
By **Hood Rich**

THE STREETS ARE CALLING
By **Duquie Wilson**

STEADY MOBBN' 1-3
THE STREETS STAINED MY SOUL 1-3
By **Marcellus Allen**

WHO SHOT YA 1-3
SON OF A DOPE FIEND 1-4
HEAVEN GOT A GHETTO 1&2
SKI MASK MONEY 1&2
By **Renta**

GORILLAZ IN THE BAY 1-4
TEARS OF A GANGSTA 1/&2
3X KRAZY 1&2
STRAIGHT BEAST MODE 1&2
By **DE'KARI**

TRIGGADALE 1-3
MURDA WAS THE CASE 1-3
By **Elijah R. Freeman**

SLAUGHTER GANG 1-3
RUTHLESS HEART 1-3
By **Willie Slaughter**

GOD BLESS THE TRAPPERS 1-3
THESE SCANDALOUS STREETS 1-3
FEAR MY GANGSTA 1-5
THESE STREETS DON'T LOVE NOBODY 1-2
BURY ME A G 1-5
A GANGSTA'S EMPIRE 1-4
THE DOPEMAN'S BODYGAURD 1&2
THE REALEST KILLAZ 1-3
THE LAST OF THE OGS 1-3
By **Tranay Adams**

MARRIED TO A BOSS 1-3
By **Destiny Skai & Chris Green**

KINGZ OF THE GAME 1-7
CRIME BOSS 1-4
By **Playa Ray**

FUK SHYT
By **Blakk Diamond**

DON'T F#CK WITH MY HEART 1&2
By **Linnea**

ADDICTED TO THE DRAMA 1-3
IN THE ARM OF HIS BOSS
By **Jamila**

LOYALTY AIN'T PROMISED 1&2
By **Keith Williams**

YAYO 1-4
A SHOOTER'S AMBITION 1&2
BRED IN THE GAME
By **S. Allen**

TRAP GOD 1-3
RICH $AVAGE 1-3
MONEY IN THE GRAVE 1-3
CARTEL MONEY 1&2
By **Martell Troublesome Bolden**

FOREVER GANGSTA 1&2
GLOCKS ON SATIN SHEETS 1&2
By **Adrian Dulan**

TOE TAGZ 1-4
LEVELS TO THIS SHYT 1&2
IT'S JUST ME AND YOU
By **Ah'Million**

TRAP STARS | B. SHELLY

KINGPIN DREAMS 1-3
RAN OFF ON DA PLUG
By **Paper Boi Rari**

THE STREETS MADE ME 1-3
By **Larry D. Wright**

CONFESSIONS OF A GANGSTA 1-4
CONFESSIONS OF A JACKBOY 1-3
CONFESSIONS OF A HITMAN
CONFESSIONS OF A DOPE BOY
By **Nicholas Lock**

I'M NOTHING WITHOUT HIS LOVE
SINS OF A THUG
TO THE THUG I LOVED BEFORE
A GANGSTA SAVED XMAS
IN A HUSTLER I TRUST
By **Monet Dragun**

QUIET MONEY 1-3
THUG LIFE 1-3
EXTENDED CLIP 1&2
A GANGSTA'S PARADISE
By **Trai'Quan**

CAUGHT UP IN THE LIFE 1-3
THE STREETS NEVER LET GO 1-3
By **Robert Baptiste**

NEW TO THE GAME 1-3
MONEY, MURDER & MEMORIES 1-3
By **Malik D. Rice**

CREAM 2-3
THE STREETS WILL TALK
By **Yolanda Moore**

THE STREETS WILL NEVER CLOSE 1-3
By **K'ajji**

LIFE OF A SAVAGE 1-4
A GANGSTA'S QUR'AN 1-4
MURDA SEASON 1-3
GANGLAND CARTEL 1-3
CHI'RAQ GANGSTAS 1-4
KILLERS ON ELM STREET 1-3
JACK BOYZ N DA BRONX 1-3
A DOPEBOY'S DREAM 1-3
JACK BOY$ VS DOPE BOYS 1-3
COKE GIRLZ
COKE BOYS
SOSA GANG 1&2
BRONX SAVAGES
BODYMORE KINGPINS
BLOOD OF A GOON
By **Romell Tukes**

CONCRETE KILLA 1-3
VICIOUS LOYALTY 1-3
BLOODY MONEY BAGS
By **Kingpen**

THE ULTIMATE SACRIFICE 1-6
KHADIFI
IF YOU CROSS ME ONCE 1-3
ANGEL 1-4
IN THE BLINK OF AN EYE
By **Anthony Fields**

THE LIFE OF A HOOD STAR
By **Ca$h & Rashia Wilson**

NIGHTMARES OF A HUSTLA 1-3
BLOOD AND GAMES 1&2
By **King Dream**

GHOST MOB
By **Stilloan Robinson**

HARD AND RUTHLESS 1&2
MOB TOWN 251
THE BILLIONAIRE BENTLEYS 1-3
REAL G'S MOVE IN SILENCE
By **Von Diesel**

MOB TIES 1-7
SOUL OF A HUSTLER, HEART OF A KILLER 1-3
GORILLAZ IN THE TRENCHES
OOPS CRY TOO 1&2
THE DAUGHTER OF A CARTEL BOSS
By **SayNoMore**

BODYMORE MURDERLAND 1-3
THE BIRTH OF A GANGSTER 1-4
By **Delmont Player**

FOR THE LOVE OF A BOSS 1&2
By **C. D. Blue**

KILLA KOUNTY 1-5
TENDER
By **Khufu**

MOBBED UP 1-4
THE BRICK MAN 1-5
THE COCAINE PRINCESS 1-10
STEPPERS 1-3
SUPER GREMLIN 1-4
A GANGSTA'S SON
By **King Rio**

MONEY GAME 1&2
By **Smoove Dolla**

TRAP STARS | B. SHELLY

A GANGSTA'S KARMA 1-5
By **FLAME**

KING OF THE TRENCHES 1-3
By **GHOST & TRANAY ADAMS**

BAD BITCHES WIT GUNZ 1&2
PROBLEM SOLVED
By "Christopher Diesel" Hornezes

QUEEN OF THE ZOO 1&2
By **Black Migo**

GRIMEY WAYS 1-3
BETRAYAL OF A G
By **Ray Vinci**

XMAS WITH AN ATL SHOOTER
By **Ca$h & Destiny Skai**

KING KILLA 1&2
By **Vincent "Vitto" Holloway**

BETRAYAL OF A THUG 1&2
By **Fre$h**

COUNTDOWN OF A KILLA 1&2
SEX, MURDER AND GOD 1&2
GUNS DOWN, BOTTOMS UP 1&2
By Lo-Life

THE MURDER QUEENS 1-7
By **Michael Gallon**

FOR THE LOVE OF BLOOD 1-4
By **Jamel Mitchell**

TRAP STARS | B. SHELLY

HOOD CONSIGLIERE 1&2
NO TIME FOR ERROR
By **Keese**

PROTÉGÉ OF A LEGEND 1,2&3
LOVE IN THE TRENCHES 1&2
By **Corey Robinson**

THE PLUG'S RUTHLESS DAUGHTER 1&2
By **Tony Daniels**

BORN IN THE GRAVE 1-3
CRIME PAYS
By **Self Made Tay**

MOAN IN MY MOUTH
By **XTASY**

TORN BETWEEN A GANGSTER AND A GENTLEMAN
By **J-BLUNT & Miss Kim**

LOYALTY IS EVERYTHING 1-3
CITY OF SMOKE 1-3
By **Molotti**

HERE TODAY GONE TOMORROW 1&2
By **Fly Rock**

WOMEN LIE MEN LIE 1-4
FIFTY SHADES OF SNOW 1-3
STACK BEFORE YOU SPLURGE
GIRLS FALL LIKE DOMINOES
NAÏVE TO THE STREETS
By **ROY MILLIGAN**

PILLOW PRINCESS
By **S. Hawkins**

TRAP STARS | B. SHELLY

THE BUTTERFLY MAFIA 1-3
SALUTE MY SAVAGERY 1&2
By **Fumiya Payne**

THE LANE 1&2
By Ken-Ken Spence

THE PUSSY TRAP 1-5
By **Nene Capri**

DIRTY DNA
By **Blaque**

SANCTIFIED AND HORNY
by **XTASY**

BOOKS BY LDP'S CEO, CA$H

TRUST IN NO MAN
TRUST IN NO MAN 2
TRUST IN NO MAN 3
BONDED BY BLOOD
SHORTY GOT A THUG
THUGS CRY
THUGS CRY 2
THUGS CRY 3
TRUST NO BITCH
TRUST NO BITCH 2
TRUST NO BITCH 3
TIL MY CASKET DROPS
RESTRAINING ORDER
RESTRAINING ORDER 2
IN LOVE WITH A CONVICT
LIFE OF A HOOD STAR
XMAS WITH AN ATL SHOOTER

www.ingramcontent.com/pod-product-compliance
Lightning Source LLC
Chambersburg PA
CBHW071214260626
47162CB00004B/1288